My Congratulations to the
"Presents" Series and to its
Readers —
   May the Romance live on!

      With my very best wishes

            Penny Jordan

Dear Reader,

Imagine if the thing you liked eating best in the world was chocolate-chip ice cream. And then imagine you tasted ice cream for a living. A dream job? Yes! Just like writing for Harlequin Presents®....

I've always loved romance—reading it *and* writing it. Love is tender, hot, anguished and joyful. Love doesn't make the world go round—it makes it spin like crazy! By reading a Harlequin Presents, you can fall in love over and over again, *without* ending up in the divorce courts!

And the best part of my job? Why, when you, dear reader, tell me how much you loved the book.

So, happy birthday, Harlequin Presents! Here's to the next twenty-five years!

Sharon Kendrick

SHARON KENDRICK

Settling the Score

Harlequin Books

TORONTO • NEW YORK • LONDON
AMSTERDAM • PARIS • SYDNEY • HAMBURG
STOCKHOLM • ATHENS • TOKYO • MILAN
MADRID • WARSAW • BUDAPEST • AUCKLAND

ISBN 0-373-11957-7

SETTLING THE SCORE

First North American Publication 1998.

Copyright © 1997 by Sharon Kendrick.

CHAPTER ONE

DOMINIC DASHWOOD drove through the ornate golden and navy gates of St Fiacre's Hill estate with just a little more speed than was necessary. Though not with as much speed as he would have *liked*, he decided, with a grim smile which nonetheless transformed his devastating features into the kind of face that most women only ever fantasised about.

Tensing one long, muscular thigh, he depressed the accelerator pedal, and his dark green Aston Martin shot forward like a bullet.

What he would have *liked* was to be on some wide, empty highway, where he could put his foot down and succumb to the heady lure of mechanical power. Machines and speed were two of Dominic's great passions. In the past women had accused him of being cold and unfeeling.

'You love that damned car more than you love me!' some sultry beauty had once poutingly accused him.

And Dominic had been unable to deny the truth which lay behind her accusation. He had taken her to bed one last time—because she had begged him to and, in truth, because he had wanted to—and had then walked away, wondering what it was that made him immune to the pain of emotion.

You know damn well what it is! mocked an inner voice, and Dominic's long fingers tightened convulsively around the soft leather of the steering wheel, as if they were biting deliciously into a woman's tender flesh. But not just *any* woman. He felt the potent flicker of desire as he slowed to take the bend near the clubhouse.

His sensual mouth twisted as a woman in tennis whites emerged from the St Fiacre's club-house. She stopped dead and stared at the car as it roared by, her eyes narrowing with speculation as they took in the hard, handsome profile of the driver.

But Dominic deliberately avoided eye contact with her. The woman's body language made it patently clear that she was available, and Dominic avoided such openly available women like the plague.

His unconscious sexual appeal had become the bane of his life. In his youth he had used it, squandered it even. For many years now he had desired the challenge of a woman who would not melt with early submission into his arms.

Unfortunately, the woman he was scheduled to meet in just under an hour was not going to provide the challenge he needed, though once again he felt the reluctant heat coursing around his veins which just the thought of her could provoke.

For Romy Salisbury was everything he despised in a woman.

She was a siren who used her sexuality indiscriminately. Who had ruined at least one man's life and had haunted his own for longer than he cared to admit.

A muscle worked in his lightly tanned cheek as he drove past another sports car, unwilling excitement shivering its way up his spine as he anticipated what he intended to happen.

Dominic smiled—but it was a cold, cruel smile as his mind lingered on the pleasure of the retribution he was going to exact in the next few days.

He had waited five years for his moment and now it had come at last.

It was high time that he settled the score with the delicious Miss Romy Salisbury.

Romy missed the turning for St Fiacre's Hill and said something rather rude underneath her breath. The entrance was so well camouflaged she was surprised that even the *residents* could find it!

But then, didn't they always say that you got what you paid for? And what St Fiacre's residents were paying for—apart from ultra-luxurious houses in the jewel-like setting of nine hundred prime Surrey acres—was privacy, pure and sweet.

Privacy from nosy tourists with their instant cameras always to hand, who were curious to know how the super-rich really lived. And privacy from good, old-fashioned fortune-hunters—people with an eye to the main chance who thought they could get rich quick by marrying into money!

Romy glanced in the rear-view mirror, realising that she would have to go right round the roundabout and come back in again.

Minutes later, she was heading back towards the St Fiacre's turn-off in her zippy little black car, bought largely with the bonus given to her by her last grateful client.

Not for the first time, Romy thanked her lucky stars that in business at least she had succeeded beyond her wildest dreams. No job was too big, too small or too difficult for Romy to tackle, and Top Class, her very own company, was going from strength to strength.

She drew up in front of the distinctive navy blue and gold wrought-iron gates which separated St Fiacre's from the rest of the world, and decided to risk a quick, critical glance at herself in the driver's mirror.

Not *too* bad, she thought dispassionately as she squinted her eyes against the glare of the sun reflected there. She flicked a trace of dust from one smooth, pale cheek and risked a closer look.

Her face carried the barest trace of make-up and her thick, straight hair was expertly styled in the urchin cut which was currently so fashionable and which made the most of the unusual pale honey colour.

She wore a silk and linen trouser suit in a neutral dark cream colour which flattered the pale magnolia of her skin and the deep velvety brown of her eyes. Beneath the suit Romy wore a simple white silk T-shirt, and she looked as she had intended to look—professional and efficient and ready for anything.

Or *anyone*, she reminded herself, with a wry little twist of her wide mouth as she punched in the security number she had been given.

The gates swung open and Romy drove through them to have her first inside view of the St Fiacre's estate.

She could see immediately why it was dubbed 'the

Beverly Hills of England' by the popular Press. It didn't just exude money—it positively *shouted* it from the summit of every beautifully designed rooftop!

Or at least what you could actually *see* of every rooftop, thought Romy as she craned her neck to try to get a better look at some of the palatial mansions she was passing.

Impossible to see *anything,* really. The hedges were too high, the gates and the fences too impenetrable. Several houses even had menacing-looking signs bearing the message "Warning! Dogs Loose!".

Romy shuddered and uttered a fervent prayer that she wouldn't bump into anything which growled and bared its teeth!

She glanced down at the directions her secretary had neatly typed out for her.

First right, down the road for half a mile, then the second house past the oak tree. She looked for confirmation that she had found the right house, saw the sign saying "Brunswick House" and, although she had tried for weeks now to suppress it, familiar cold fingers of fear crept over her skin.

Don't be crazy, she urged herself silently. It's just a job, like any other job. A job, what's more, that you could do in your sleep!

But it was so much more than a job to Romy—in fact, for once, most uncharacteristically, the job had taken on secondary importance. Not even her secretary knew how high the stakes were going to be at this particular interview. For Romy was going to see Dominic again, after five long years which had seemed to stretch out in front of her like an eternity.

And this time she intended to exorcise his cruel and sexy ghost once and for all.

The gates were open and Romy steered the car down a sweeping drive which seemed to go on for ever, dimly observing the beautifully laid out gardens in the middle of which glittered a formal lake, before drawing up in front of an elegant red-brick house.

She switched off the ignition and quietly took in her surroundings.

In front of the house a dark green Aston Martin was parked, its sleek lines lying so close to the ground that it looked like a lithe jungle cat, just before it pounced.

So he was home...

Waiting...

Suppressing a shiver, and picking up her slim leather briefcase, Romy swung her legs out of the car, wishing that she could shake off the persistent and rather disconcerting feeling that she was being watched.

She had raised one hand to press on the doorbell when the door was suddenly opened, and Romy stood staring up at a man whose coldly handsome features would be etched on her memory until her dying day.

Dominic Dashwood—in the living, breathing flesh.

And... Oh, my *God*!

Elation and despair swamped over her like a tidal wave as she discovered that time and maturity had done nothing except add to that formidable appeal of his. He had always been a dynamic-looking man, but now he exuded the quietly confident air of the *seriously* successful.

With the expertise born of weeks of practice, Romy somehow managed to present to him a face which was both polite and impassive, as if he were just another client she was meeting.

'Hello,' he said softly.

'H-hello,' she stammered, feeling as overcome as a sixteen-year-old in the presence of her favourite pop star. Oh, *why* in heaven's name had she agreed to take the job? Had she really been stupid enough to think that she might now be immune to him? After all that had happened between them?

So what did she do next? Did she pretend she didn't recognise him, or what? She hunted for the smallest flicker of recognition in *his* eyes but saw nothing other than self-possession and detachment. So either he *didn't* recognise her or he was pretending not to. Well, two could play at that game, mister!

'Romy Salisbury,' he stated, in a deep voice which still had the power to bring her out in goosebumps beneath the cream jacket she wore. His steely grey eyes swept over her in candid assessment.

Romy waited, but that was all he said and she carefully kept her face neutral—determined not to show that she was *itching* to know why he had asked her here.

It might simply be coincidence that he had hired her, of course. She was, after all, one of the best party planners in the business. So why on earth look for hidden agendas which might simply not exist? And wouldn't it be best for everyone if he *didn't* recognise her? Five years was a long time.

But deep in her heart she knew that it was not

coincidence which had brought her here this weekend. Men like Dominic Dashwood did not allow something as unpredictable as coincidence to govern their lives.

'That's right,' she agreed with a smile, and decided to follow his lead—polite but distant.

Very distant.

'So, by a simple process of elimination, you must be...' Her voice faltered slightly as she failed to block out just how spectacularly handsome he was. How could she have forgotten *that*? 'Austen Holdings, I suppose?' she finished pertly, giving the name of the company in which he had made the booking, presumably to keep *his* identity secret.

She held her hand out to him, triumphant in the knowledge that in *that* at least he had failed! 'So would you prefer me to call you Austen?' she enquired sweetly. 'Or Holdings?'

Dominic had to bite back a reluctant smile as he wondered if her cool indifference was feigned or genuine; his pride and his ego instinctively rebelled against the unthinkable—that she did not remember him!

But he hesitated for no more than a fraction of a second, then took her outstretched hand in his. 'You must call me Dominic,' he instructed softly. 'Or Dashwood, if you prefer.'

His grey eyes blazed at her as he watched for her reaction, and this made Romy even more determined to keep her face impassive.

'Dominic will do just fine,' she agreed noncommittally. 'Why on earth should I want to call you Dashwood?'

He smiled, but now Romy could detect a cold flicker of anger which lurked in the depths of his grey eyes. Had her supposed failure to recognise him provoked that? she wondered.

'Because the new wave of women seem to rather enjoy calling men by their surnames,' he explained, his deep voice sounding faintly steely. 'Maybe it reminds them of their schooldays—or maybe it just gives them a feeling of power over the opposite sex,' he concluded, his eyes glittering with an unspoken question.

But Romy couldn't think straight enough to answer any question, unspoken or otherwise. Because his handshake assumed an air of almost shocking intimacy as she felt that first brief caress.

The sensation of having him grasp her fingers like that made her mouth fall open in an instinctive gasp, and she remembered just how intimately those hands had explored every centimetre of her body... She had to battle to stop herself from swaying.

'Are you feeling ill?' His eyes narrowed and he let her hand go, but he hadn't missed the darkening of her eyes and the swift hardening of her nipples beneath the silken T-shirt, and Dominic felt a small but triumphant surge of sexual power heating his loins.

His voice sounded concerned, but Romy didn't miss the speculative gleam in those steely grey eyes.

'No. I'm just—hot.' She indicated the blazing sun with a wave of her arm. 'That's all.'

He nodded. 'Of course you are,' he agreed formally. 'Hot and bothered. It's been the hottest July on record. So why don't we go inside and I can fix you something cool to drink while we discuss the job?'

Romy was horribly aware that he automatically seemed to be taking control of the situation, and found herself wondering just why she was allowing it to happen.

Romy's whole life was her job. She was a party planner, or an "entertainment expert" as she preferred to call it! She took the sting out of organising any function—from the smallest children's birthday tea to the grandest weekend shooting party.

She spent the majority of her time working in other people's homes, from huge and austere Scottish castles to the most opulent of London residences, and she had never suffered a single qualm about the nature of her work in the past.

So why did she now feel as though she was some poor, unsuspecting little fly being lured into the web of an evil black spider?

And why the hell didn't he say something about what had happened between the two of them five years earlier? About the man she had gone on to marry?

Feeling weak and more than a little shaky, Romy followed him through a long, echoing hallway and into an airy sitting room which overlooked a garden bright with summer flowers. Even further into the distance shone the golden dazzle of sunlight as it glanced off the waters of the lake.

'Please sit,' he suggested, though he did no such thing himself, moving to stand by the elegant stone fireplace and surveying her with a cool watchfulness, an insulting and almost icy detachment in his face which Romy suddenly longed to smash into smithereens.

'Thanks.' She perched on the edge of a yellow damask chaise lounge before turning towards him. Taking all her courage into her hands, she drew in a very deep breath and said, 'So just why have you invited me here today, Dominic?'

An ironic twist of the lips she remembered so well was the only outward reaction to her remark. 'Ah! So you *do* recognise me?'

She gave him a bitter, brittle smile. 'Don't be so ridiculous! Of course I recognise you!'

'Well, *that's* a relief,' he observed, with sardonic emphasis.

'Or do you imagine for a moment that I always have—'

'Sex with complete strangers in lifts?' he supplied drily.

An angry flare of colour emphasised Romy's high cheekbones. 'I did *not* have sex with you!' she protested huskily.

'No? Depends on your definition of sex, surely?' he queried insultingly. 'It's true we stopped short of actual—'

'Stop it!' Romy yelled, and actually clapped her hands over her ears, but dropped them almost immediately when she realised how childish the gesture must appear.

'Why?' he questioned, in mock surprise. 'Does it bother you?'

'Of course it bothers me!' she declared.

'What does?' he snapped. 'Your indiscriminate sexual appetite? Or your cuckolding of the man who was my best friend?'

'And what about *you*, Dominic?' she retorted, trying to resist the thrill it gave her just to say his name out loud. 'Does it make you feel good to know that hours before you were due to be best man at our wedding you were practically ripping off my underwear?'

'*Ripping* it off?' he drawled arrogantly. 'I think your memory must be defective, Romy. As I recall, we didn't actually remove *any* of your clothes, did we? But I suspect that you would have needed very little coaxing to do so! Don't you? Be honest now.'

Her cheeks still on fire, Romy shut her eyes, as if that would dispel the tantalising and forbidden pictures which had sprung up before her mind's eye with disturbing clarity. And when she opened them again she surprised a taut, angry mask which had momentarily hardened his features. So he was tense, too, was he? she thought with surprise. Then why? Why bring her here? 'That's all water under the bridge now, surely?' she asked him.

His eyes were piercing, their silver-grey light as direct and as steely as a sword. 'Is it? I find that I tend to file the whole episode away under "unfinished business" rather than "water under the bridge".'

'Perhaps that's your conscience troubling you?' Romy suggested sweetly, and then immediately wished she hadn't.

'Perhaps it is.' His eyes were icy cold. 'And what about *your* conscience, Romy? Does that ever give *you* a sleepless night? Do you ever think about

Mark? Did you think about Mark as you made those false wedding vows—?'

'They were *not* false!' she declared automatically.

'Those false wedding vows,' he persisted, with deadly calm. 'Just hours after I felt you climax beneath my fingers.' He shook his head, as if he had been given an insurmountable problem to solve. 'It still seems scarcely credible to me that the supposedly virgin bride my college friend had spoken of so proudly and so fondly should have been grappling half-naked with me within minutes of our meeting.'

But it wasn't like that! Romy would have yelled at him, if he hadn't literally taken her breath away with his candour. Nothing like that!

Except that he wouldn't believe her—and why should he? There was a whacking great kernel of truth behind his words. She had done *all* those things he had accused her of—and more! And if she tried to defend her actions she would sound like the worst kind of hypocrite—the kind of woman who allowed herself to get carried away by passion and then turned around and blamed the man.

No, if there was any blame to be apportioned then it must be laid firmly at her door. After all, Dominic had not forced her to do anything she had not wanted to. Quite the contrary, in fact...

Dominic stared at her and frowned. Her face had gone as white as a glass of milk and she had started to sway. Instinctively, he moved away from the fireplace and was beside her in seconds, his hands gripping at her upper arms beneath the soft material of her jacket.

'Romy?' he demanded roughly, the soft feel of her flesh beneath his hands making him want to do something much more elemental than comfort her. 'Are you OK?'

The way he said her name was like cool water to a thirsty camel, the touch of his hands like some rejuvenating life-force, and Romy found herself staring helplessly into his eyes.

Close up, his presence haunted her even more. Initially she had thought that he had changed very little, but she had been wrong. It was true that the thick ruffled hair had remained untouched by grey—a fact made all the more remarkable by its coal-dark blackness—but the years had subtly redefined his face, Romy realised. All the softness of youth had completely disappeared. His features were harder, while his mouth fell naturally into a cynical line. Around the piercing grey eyes were now the fine lines of age and experience. He looked, she thought, suppressing a sudden shudder of sexual awareness, like a man who knew exactly what he wanted out of life...

So what the hell did he want from *her*?

'Romy!' he said again, and this time gave her an almost imperceptible little shake. 'What is it?'

She stared at him, completely deflated by the shocking memory of what had happened between the two of them. 'I'm tired.'

'Tired?' He gave a cynical laugh. 'I'm not surprised! Deception *can* be tiring, can't it? In fact, it must be positively *exhausting*. Imagine the amount of devious planning it must take to make sure that your lies don't get found out. I wonder if Mark ever found you out?' he mused. 'I often wonder if your rampant promiscuity could have been a contributing factor to his premature death.'

Romy sucked in an agonised breath, a movement which made her cheekbones look impossibly hollow. How *could* he? How could he be so deliberately cruel? But she decided to let it go. For the moment.

'Quite apart from the fact that your sexual demands must have been pretty challenging,' he continued contemptuously, 'I must say that even I have never met a woman who was turned on so completely or so quickly as you, Romy. I don't think that Mark was the best man to be able to cope with your needs, do you?'

'That's enough!' she told him angrily, shaking his hands off her arms impatiently. He had only pretended to be concerned—it had taken very little time for him to start insulting her all over again! 'Don't you imagine I feel bad enough about Mark's death without you adding to it with your vile accusations?'

His eyes glittered with dangerous challenge. 'So your conscience is entirely clear, is it, Romy?'

'Oh, *damn* you, Dominic Dashwood!' She could barely bring herself to look into those clever, searching silver eyes. 'Damn you to hell!' And as her words whipped discordantly around the room Romy wondered just what her secretary would say if she could hear her.

Or see her. Sitting weakly and pathetically on the edge of the sofa whilst glaring balefully at a man who was doing nothing more sensational than recounting facts which she had tried to keep hidden away—even from herself—for all these years.

What the hell was happening to her? Romy Salisbury was famous for her ability to remain unruffled, for refusing to be thrown—no matter how sticky the situation.

What about the time early last year, for example, when a foreign minor royal had hired her to organise an American evening for his thirty-fifth birthday and the cook and the waitress had failed to show?

Romy had cooked and served the meal entirely by herself, and the royal personage had got wind of it, insisting on coming down into the kitchen to congratulate her in person.

'Oh, it was nothing, sir.' Romy had blushed modestly, whilst trying out a very rusty curtsy. 'Just hot dogs and beans and a mud-pie pudding.'

'Though I suspect,' the Prince had murmured, with a practised smile, 'that even a swan fashioned out of ice would not have defeated you!'

'I'm just grateful that you had less elaborate requirements than that, sir!' Romy had joked, pulling a mock grimace which had told the Prince exactly what she thought of over-the-top gestures like swans made out of ice. And the twinkle in the Prince's eye had told her that he agreed with her sentiments entirely!

After that, her workload had quadrupled overnight, giving Romy the luxury of being able to pick and choose her jobs. It really was amazing how much clout royal patronage gave you!

So, this Romy Salisbury who could chat with ease

to princes—what connection did she have with the woman who was currently behaving like a beaten dog? Just because she had come across the man she had alternately dreamed of and dreaded meeting for five long years. What are you, Romy Salisbury? she asked herself. A woman or a wimp?

Her dark eyes flared with the light of battle, and Dominic's eyes raked over her face.

'So why?' he suddenly demanded.

So many whys. 'I'm not a mind-reader!' she retorted. 'Why what?'

'Why did you pretend not to recognise me?'

Romy smiled and decided to brazen it out. 'Because I dislike the idea of being manipulated, I suppose.'

'Manipulated?'

'That's right.'

'Manipulated by whom?'

'Don't sound so surprised,' she remonstrated tartly. 'By you, of course. You deliberately went to the trouble of booking me under the name of one of your more obscure property companies instead of giving your *real* name. Presumably with the intention of shocking me when we met. What kind of reaction were you hoping for, Dominic? That I would collapse in a swoon at your feet when I came face to face with you?'

His grey eyes narrowed. 'You mean you *knew* that you were about to meet me?'

'Of course I knew!' scoffed Romy. 'Or did you imagine that I would just happily take a job without bothering to check it out first? My work involves me going into people's homes—often staying there. *And*

I'm a woman! Do you suppose for a moment that I would put myself at risk by not finding out a few details about who is employing me? I'm running a business here, Dominic, for heaven's sake, not a knitting circle!'

He gave her a grudging look of admiration. 'Well, well, well, Romy,' he observed drily. 'You seem to have acquired a little common sense over the years, at least. Pity it didn't come five years earlier.'

His patronising comment made Romy even more angry. She drew a deep, indignant breath. 'But even if I *hadn't* known I was going to meet you, why would you naturally assume that I'd recognise you immediately? Is it so inconceivable that I would fail to do so? Do you imagine that you are such a magnificent specimen, Dominic, that you're unforgettable? That any woman meeting you would have you branded indelibly on her memory for evermore?'

'I would have been more than a little—surprised if you had failed to recognise me. Quite apart from the fact that I was your best man. After all, we had quite an…experience together, didn't we?' He gave a lazy smile which made Romy uncomfortably aware that he was recalling that erotic encounter in the lift. 'Though I have to admit that most women tell me I have an unforgettable face.'

His words stabbed at her like a knife and it took every ounce of concentration that Romy possessed not to lash out at him in a jealous fit of rage she knew she had no right to feel.

'Oh, *do* they?'

'Yes.' He smiled arrogantly. 'They do.'

'Dominic Dashwood,' Romy declared heatedly, 'did anyone ever tell you that you are nothing but an arrogant...arrogant...?'

'Bastard?' he supplied drily. 'Is that the word you're searching for? So why not come out and say it, Romy? It's true, after all.'

Romy gave him a steady look. 'I would have used a far more creative insult than "bastard", thank you very much! And that sounds like a mighty big chip on your shoulder to me.'

His smile had suddenly died and now he shook his dark head with slow emphasis. 'Not at all,' he said thoughtfully. 'Illegitimacy no longer carries the stigma that it did when I was growing up.'

She stared at him in surprise. Surely that wasn't a trace of vulnerability showing through the steely armour?

Romy had always defined Dominic as a black-hearted villain and seducer. But now, with the benefit of maturity, she recognised that she might have been guilty of a little over-simplification.

Had he been a victim of taunts at school? Ridiculed and derided as a child because he had been born on the wrong side of the blanket?

For the first time she lost something of her guarded expression. Her mouth softened and her lips moved into an unconscious pout as a wave of empathy washed over her.

What was it about this man, she wondered, that she should want to take him in her arms and comfort him? And after everything that had happened between them, too...

She gazed across the room at him, the sudden silence making her acutely aware of their isolation.

Her mind began to stray into forbidden territory as she allowed her eyes to drift over the magnificent thrust of his thighs, all tensile muscular perfection beneath the cambric trousers. And the thin silk shirt he wore did absolutely everything to emphasise the hard, lean abdomen and the suggestion of strength rippling in each arm.

Romy shut her eyes in despair, and when she opened them it was to find him staring at her.

'We'd better have something to drink,' he said abruptly. 'You look terrible.'

'You don't look so wonderful yourself,' she lied, but she found herself sinking back against the chaise lounge. Because he was right. She *felt* terrible. The shock of seeing him again, no doubt. And making the disappointing discovery that in five years she had built up no magic immunity against his devastating appeal.

His eyes narrowed as they raked over her slumped frame. 'Stay there!' he ordered curtly.

'I'm not going anywhere,' she murmured drily.

Their eyes locked for one long moment, and when he turned to leave Romy found herself watching his retreat obsessively, unable to tear her eyes away from him and yet despising her need to do so.

When Romy had met him he had been twenty-six— very bright and very ambitious. It had been easy, then, to predict that he had a golden future ahead of him. But now it was possible to see how he had managed to surpass even that early promise.

And it wasn't so much the palatial mansion he lived

in, or the expensive clothes he wore, or even the tell-tale designer watch which was designed to withstand almost anything and had a price tag to match. No, it was something much less tangible than material possessions, and yet far more valuable in its way.

For Dominic carried a quiet authority about him which combined both strength and dignity.

He was, Romy recognised, the type of man whose respect would be highly valued. And there was no doubt in her mind that he would probably accord more respect to a snail than he would to her.

And could she blame him? Could she? If she told even the most impartial observer the facts concerning their ill-fated meeting, would they not condemn her, too?

She tried to stem them, but the memories were too strong, too long suppressed for her to be able to stop them flooding back with bitter-sweet clarity.

Long-forgotten fragments of events floated free and her mind took her back to a summer's afternoon almost exactly five years before...

CHAPTER TWO

IT WAS the afternoon before her wedding, and Romy was feeling sick.

The make-up artist had just been through a trial run before tomorrow's church service, and had put far more gunge on her face than she was used to. Romy peered in the mirror and frowned. The oodles of mascara and foundation might have made her eyes look bigger and her skin even smoother, but she looked much *older*. And harder, too.

So she went straight into the bathroom and scrubbed the whole lot off!

Her mother was lying on the bed in the hotel room, drinking unchilled white wine and stuffing cotton-wool balls between her toes as she waited for the red varnish on her nails to dry.

She looked up as Romy entered the room, and frowned. 'Put some make-up on!' she ordered instantly. 'Your face looks awful without it!'

Ignoring that, Romy sat down on the edge of her bed and studied her fingernails intently. 'Do you—do you think every bride feels like this?' she asked her mother tentatively.

Her mother took another swig of warm wine. 'Like what?'

Romy swallowed as she struggled to explain her thoughts to her mother—although she supposed that there was absolutely no reason why she should suddenly succeed after all these years. 'Oh, I don't know. Excited, I suppose, and yet…well, *afraid*, too…'

Stella Salisbury, whose dissolute life was finally taking its toll on her once beautiful face, shot her daughter an acid look. 'All I can remember is the feeling of being shackled,' she drawled, and lit a cigarette. 'But unfortunately there wasn't a lot I could do about it—I was pregnant with you at the time.'

'Mum…' Romy sighed worriedly. 'Do you really think you *need* any more to drink? There'll be plenty at the party tonight. And you want to be sober for *that*, don't you?'

'Why?' asked her mother, inhaling deeply on her cigarette. 'It's hardly likely to be the bash of the year, now, is it? Honestly, Romy, I didn't spend all that money on your education for you to marry the first man who asked you! The Ackroyds may be a fine, old-established family—but they're as dull as ditchwater!'

And that's precisely why I'm marrying Mark, thought Romy as she helplessly watched her mother refilling her glass. Because he's everything that you're not and he wants to give me everything I've never had.

In a nutshell, Mark represented security. And Romy craved security with all the fervour of someone who had spent her formative years being bundled from pillar to post while her mother worked her way through a series of unsuitable boyfriends. Romy's father had been killed in Africa when she was just a tiny baby, and she had never known a single, stabilising male influence.

'Besides…' Stella fixed her daughter with a sharp look '…there might not even *be* a wedding at this rate!'

Romy pushed a strand of blonde hair out of her eye. 'What do you mean?' she asked in alarm.

Stella shrugged. 'Well, the best man still hasn't arrived, has he? And it beats me why a man with Mark Ackroyd's connections has chosen someone who nobody knows from Adam. Someone told me that he grew up on completely the wrong side of the tracks, so why on earth—'

'Because he saved Mark's life when they were at Oxford,' put in Romy patiently. 'I thought I'd explained that.'

'Then why isn't he here?'

'He's flying over from Hong Kong. He works there. He'll arrive tomorrow morning. The wedding's not until three, so there will be plenty of time.'

'Cutting it a little fine, isn't he? What if he's delayed?'

Romy shrugged. 'He won't be.'

'What do you mean, "He won't be"?'

'Just that Mark says that when Dominic says he'll do something then we are to consider it done.' She coughed, her nostrils filling with the smoke from her mother's cigarette, which hung in a foul-smelling grey fog in the hotel room. 'It's so smoky in here!' she spluttered, flapping her hand around in an effort to dispel it.

'It's a dump!' retorted Stella, looking around the room with a grimace.

'It is *not* a dump!' protested Romy automatically.

'Why we're staying here I simply *don't* know!' shrilled Mrs Salisbury. 'Not when your husband-to-be owns the biggest house in the entire county.'

Because Romy had put her foot down very firmly—that was why! She suppressed a shudder as she tried to imagine her mother and Mark's mother sharing the same house, even for one night! 'You get your freedom here,' she said, looking meaningfully at the overflowing ashtray and the half-empty bottle of wine.

Though perhaps if Stella had been treated to the rather abstemious hospitality of the formidable Mrs Ackroyd, then she might have applied the brakes a bit. And subsequently have been in a better state for tonight's party!

Romy sighed, wishing that the ceremony was already over, and it was just her and Mark.

And?

She swallowed.

It was normal to feel pre-wedding nerves, perfectly normal—she had to accept that. And Mark was so very proud of the fact that she was a virgin.

'So many girls aren't these days,' he had told her fondly, planting a tender kiss on her long neck. 'That's why I want to keep you pure and innocent for as long as possible!'

Romy impatiently pushed another lock of hair off her suddenly hot face. 'I'm going out for a while!' she told her mother abruptly.

'Out? Now? But you can't! What about the party?'

'The party isn't for hours,' answered Romy, with an oddly detached kind of calm. 'And I'm afraid I'll have little stomach for it if I sit around here watching you get steadily sozzled. So why don't you order up some black coffee, Mum, and try to get a little sleep?'

Barely registering her mother's amazement at the fact that she had answered her back, Romy left the hotel room without a backward glance.

She hesitated outside the door, not quite sure where she intended going. A walk, perhaps. Yes, that was it! A walk in the brilliant July sunshine—that might help her shake off this curiously unsettled mood. Besides, there was nothing else for her to do except fill in the empty hours.

Everything was ready and waiting for the Big Day. The white tulle dress was hanging in the wardrobe swathed in thick plastic. The white satin shoes were lined up neatly below, and frothy little flounces of white lace underwear lay in neat, snowy piles.

Romy automatically quickened her step as she walked towards the smaller lift at the end of the tenth-floor corridor, instinctively avoiding the main lift. Lots of the wedding guests were also staying at the hotel and she didn't want to run into any of them. Because for some reason Romy couldn't face talking, not to anyone, not just now...

She pressed the button and waited, and presently the lift doors jerked open and she stepped inside, pressed the button for the ground floor and it began its descent.

On the seventh floor the doors opened and a man entered, a man so drop-dead gorgeous that Romy actually blinked distractedly as she stared at him.

He stared right back—so intently and with such a

piercing expression in a pair of exceptional silver-grey eyes that all Romy's usual defences crumbled, and she was left feeling curiously exposed and vulnerable.

Hastily she started studying the carpet with the kind of avid interest she usually reserved for the gossip column in her favourite newspaper!

But, try as she might to concentrate on the swirly red and gold pattern, she found herself unable to stop observing him from out of the corner of her eye, even though she pretended not to.

He looked to be in his mid-twenties, and was impressively tall, with hair which was as dark as coal. He had powerfully built shoulders and his skin was lightly tanned, so that it made a flattering contrast against the pale linen suit he wore.

But it was his face which was truly remarkable— angular and hypnotic, its hard, flat planes casting intriguing shadows. The mouth was a contradiction, in that it had full, curved lines which hinted at an experience Romy did not dare dwell on, but already there was a hard, cynical twist in place. And that was surprising in one so young, she thought fleetingly.

He looked up and caught her peeping, and his grey eyes flicked over her with unashamed interest. He gave a brief, knowing smile, before turning his attention back to the folded-up copy of the financial paper he was carrying.

Romy couldn't concentrate. Or, rather, she could— but on one thing and one thing alone.

That man!

As the lift continued its descent she found herself so acutely aware of his presence that it was almost painful. But then he was an exceptionally good-looking man, she reasoned, and her reaction was perfectly natural. Just because she was getting married the next day, that did not mean that she would never find another man attractive!

Nevertheless, she found herself praying that the lift would quickly reach its destination.

It did—but it was not the one she had been counting on! In between floors five and six it made a sickening kind of screeching noise and then juddered to a deafeningly silent halt.

Nervously, Romy lifted her hand and started jabbing at the button several times, but the lift remained stubbornly stuck, and when she dared to look up at the man it was to find him observing her, a wry smile on his lips making her quickly revise her earlier opinion of him. Not exceptionally good-looking, she concluded, but *outrageously* good-looking!

'And you thought that this kind of thing only happened in films, didn't you?' he said.

Romy didn't answer, just continued to punch away at the lift button with a desperation she did not quite like to analyse.

'If you don't mind my saying so,' he observed, in that same deep and drawling voice, 'bashing the thing is likely to do more harm than good!'

'Then what do you suggest I do?' she snapped back.

He raised a lazy black brow. 'You could try pressing the alarm button,' he suggested.

Now why hadn't *she* thought of that?

Feeling more than a bit of a fool, Romy did just

that, disappointed and yet not surprised when nothing happened.

He moved forward and began studying the buttons, pressing each one experimentally at first and then trying different combinations, like someone struggling to find the right password on a strange computer. But, no matter what he did, the lift remained stubbornly still.

The man frowned. 'Could be the electrics, I suppose, as the alarm isn't working either,' he commented thoughtfully. 'Although we still have light, so maybe the mechanism is on a completely different circuit.'

For some reason, his calm assurance infuriated her. And so did the fact that she couldn't understand a word he was saying!

'Is that all you can say?' she demanded, her voice rising with every word. 'Standing there wittering on about electrics when we're stuck in this lift—*alone*!'

'Not alone. *Together*,' he corrected her, and gave her a narrow-eyed look. 'And if you continue to get hysterical—'

'I am *not* getting hysterical!'

'Yes, you are!' he chided gently.

'I'll get hysterical if I want to!' she yelled. 'Who *wouldn't* get hysterical if they were stuck in a lift with a complete stranger?'

He gave a lazy smile, the corners of his mouth turning up in a way which suddenly made Romy's heart thunder as it had never thundered before.   'Do I make you nervous, then?' he queried wickedly.

'Yes, you jolly well do! And I'm certainly not going to accept this false imprisonment lying down!'

It was the worst thing she could have said, and the answering glint of light in his grey eyes made her fervently wish that she could rephrase that last statement!

'What a pity,' he murmured.

'In fact, I'm going to yell for help!' she announced wildly, saying anything—*anything*—to stop him looking at her in that way... She glared at him challengingly.

'Be my guest,' he drawled, and carelessly loosened the tie of cornflower silk which was knotted around his throat. 'Yell to your heart's content, sweetheart!'

Sticking her mouth as close to the door as possible, Romy shouted, *'Help!'* at the top of her voice, and listened as the word echoed its way down the silent lift shaft. She drew in a deep breath for another attempt. *'Help!'* But again her shout simply echoed into nothingness, and the lack of response made Romy's heart race with real fear.

'Why don't *you* yell for help?' she challenged.

'Because there's no one out there to hear us,' he pointed out reasonably. 'It's a little-used lift. We would do much better to wait until we hear someone banging around, and *then* yell!'

'And what if we never get out?' she babbled, moving forward and clutching onto his lapels with white-knuckled fingers, her voice rising to a high, brittle note which threatened to crack. She buckled against him. 'What if we die of thirst, or starve to death?'

'We won't,' he soothed, and almost absently

stroked the blonde hair which was now resting against his chest. 'We'll be just *fine.*'

She quickly dropped her hands from where they were busy creasing the linen of his lapels! 'No, we won't! We'll be stuck here for ever! I just *know* we will! I—'

He lifted her chin with his forefinger so that she could not escape that blazing, stormy gaze. 'The classic remedy for hysteria is a slap to the face.' He cut across her words with a frown which gradually gave way to a slow, careful smile. 'But I'm not inclined to do that. For a start, it's such a beautiful face...'

The softness in his deep voice instantly and magically diffused all the terror she felt. A beautiful face? Romy went pink with pleasure at the compliment, and then immediately started thinking how *pathetic* she must look! And should he really be saying something like that to an engaged woman?

But when she threw a covert glance down at her left hand she discovered that she had left her engagement ring lying on the dressing table in the hotel room. There was no outward symbol to show the world she was spoken for. So she had better start *acting* like a mature woman who was about to be married!

Fixing her most intelligent look on her face, she drew a deep, calming breath and said steadily, 'And how do you propose we get out of here?'

He stared down at her intently, his face and body suddenly tense. His eyes were cold and grey, Romy noted with a shiver—as hard and as glittering as a blade of steel.

Romy instantly became aware that all normal sounds had been deadened—muffled by the pulses which thundered in her head. Her line of vision had contracted to one small area, and she found that all she could see were the firm, sensual curves of his mouth.

He seemed to move fractionally towards her, and for one heart-stopping moment she actually thought that he was about to bend that dark, gorgeous head to kiss her—and found that she was holding her breath, waiting and anticipating his next move.

Then suddenly he laughed, and shifted his weight rather awkwardly, as though he was uncomfortable. 'I'm afraid I don't have any immediate solution. So we'll just have to wait. Sooner or later someone is bound to notice that one of us is missing or that the lift is firmly stuck between floors.'

'Of course,' she said stiffly, and deliberately turned her back on him, feeling absolutely mortified—aware that for a moment back then she had very much wanted him to kiss her. Had he been aware of her wish, too?

Was that another sign of pre-wedding nerves? she wondered worriedly. Wanting total strangers to pull you into their arms and to kiss you to within about an inch of your life? Tight-lipped, she stared at the blank wall, feeling disgusted with herself.

Dominic looked at the tense set of her shoulders, his mouth hardening as he recognised the hypnotic pull of sexual attraction which was building up in the confined space with all the speed of cells multiplying.

He tried to rationalise the situation. He had given

little time or thought to pleasure over the past year, and this overwhelming need to crush her against him was probably just his body's reaction to such self-imposed denial.

He had been working flat out for months and months, taking on a job in a law firm in Hong Kong for which he had been much too young and too unqualified, but in which he had absolutely triumphed—to everyone's astonishment bar his own.

For Dominic was determined to succeed, to be the first member of his family who didn't live in fear of the bailiffs.

He had grown up in poverty—real, abject poverty—with a mother who was proud and hard enough to let her only child go hungry. And Dominic had never forgotten hunger. Memories of that great aching emptiness gnawing away at the pit of his stomach had driven him on and on. He had vowed to stop only when he had made enough never to have to worry about hunger again.

The only trouble was that he had reached that stage a long time ago, but had blinded himself to the fact.

His whole life was work. Women did not feature in his grand scheme of things. Women distracted you with their beguiling eyes and their soft bodies. And women like this one—with her honey-blonde hair rippling like moonbeams over pert, high young breasts—well… Dominic could imagine never wanting to work again if he lost himself in *her* arms.

Oh, he dated occasionally—but in relationships he could control. Completely. And for this reason his affairs usually tended to be with older women.

Women who knew the score. Women in their early thirties, with established careers of their own, who were not looking for a permanent partner. Or, at least, that was what they always told him at the beginning. Three months down the line, when they started talking babies and houses, Dominic would be forced to end the relationship as gently as possible.

Settling down was simply not an option at this time in his life and he sometimes wondered whether it ever would be. For he had never known happiness or security in his own childhood and so had no idea how to create it.

He shifted his weight as he felt the uncomfortable heaviness of desire building up, but unfortunately there was nowhere to look at that moment, except at the source of that desire.

His eyes lingered reluctantly on the pure, clean sweep of her neck. Noted the way her simple blue T-shirt and denim mini-skirt flowed down over her slim, healthy curves. God, but she looked so young and so beautiful! And so impossibly innocent, too!

But innocent she could not be, he decided grimly—not from the way she had looked at him just now. He had surprised a wide-eyed look of pure invitation on her face. This happened to Dominic with such monotonous regularity that it usually left him cold, however beautiful the woman. And yet for some reason, with *this* woman, it was taking every bit of will-power he possessed not to succumb to it.

Romy had started to feel hot. Tiny pinpricks of heat began to scratch irritatingly at her forehead, and surreptitiously she drew the back of her hand across it.

'Perhaps we should sit down,' he suggested.

She turned, suddenly aware of how close he was, the scent of him invading her nostrils like the sweetest perfume. 'Wh-why?'

'Because it's hot and stressful in here.' *Very* stressful, he thought ruefully as he watched the tiny pulse at her temple beat so frantically. 'Confined space, and all that. Aren't we supposed to conserve oxygen and energy in such a situation? I don't want you fainting on me.'

Romy smiled. 'Do I look like the fainting type?'

He narrowed his eyes. 'You look…delicate, if you must know. Too pale with those shadows bruising your eyes—as if you haven't been sleeping much lately.'

'I'm sorry I asked!' she joked, but she slid to the floor as he had suggested, and looked rather pointedly at the space beside her. 'But if all you say is true, then shouldn't you be joining me?'

As soon as Dominic saw her coltish young legs sprawled in front of her, he knew he had made a mistake. A *big* mistake. He tried to will the desire away, but by now it was in such an advanced state that it stubbornly refused to go.

And she was right; he really *ought* to join her. Standing was no help to his discomfort at all. From here he had a too tantalising view of what her breasts might be like if they were bare. Whenever she moved, the thin blue material of her T-shirt moved fractionally with her—so that he caught an occasional

glimpse of the creamy flesh above the luscious swell
of her breasts.

He reluctantly crouched down and arranged his
long-legged frame in the cramped space with difficulty. And found that sitting beside her was the only
sensible way to stop him from staring at her more than
was absolutely necessary.

'Are you frightened?' he asked her conversation-
ally, in an effort to distract himself from the rapid
rising and falling of her breasts as she tried her best
to act unconcerned by his proximity.

'I'm not sure,' she hedged, because she found it
difficult to lie, and in truth she was very frightened
indeed—though more by the intensity of her body's
reaction to a man who was a complete stranger than
by her entrapment.

She could feel the heat pricking her skin, the insis-
tent peaking of her nipples beneath the gossamer-fine
lace of the bra she wore. 'Are you?' she asked, more
urgently than she had intended. 'Frightened?'

He barely heard her. His thoughts were all taken
up with the dewy appearance of her skin. He found
himself mesmerised by the fine beads of sweat which
were beginning to mist the magnolia-pale area beneath her neck. 'Am I what?' he asked her distractedly.

'Frightened.'

He found himself mesmerised by her eyes now.
Great big pixie eyes—as rich and dark as the most
expensive chocolate. He leaned forward, unable to
stop himself, and removed a non-existent speck of
dust from her nose. He saw her begin to shiver vio-

lently, as though she was unable to control herself, and he was suddenly overwhelmed by a sensation of inevitability which was almost *primitive* in its intensity.

The air crackled; the silence was like thunder in their ears.

'No,' he said firmly. 'Fear is just about the last thing on my mind right now.'

'D-don't.' She stumbled over the word, even though he was no longer touching her, but the grey eyes were suddenly blazing into hers with a fervent silvery fire which thrilled her.

'Don't what?' he queried, so neutrally that the question seemed to pose no threat. 'Don't marvel at your exquisite beauty—when not to do so would be a crime? Or don't kiss you—when we both know that's what you want more than anything else in the world right now?' His voice deepened to a husky caress. 'What we *both* want,' he finished.

'You—*can't*,' Romy breathed in thrilled disbelief. 'You can't just come out and say things like *that*!'

'Oh, I think I can,' he contradicted her, with a glittering and arrogant confidence which renewed the racing of her heart.

And then the lights went out.

Instinct made her leap into his arms, and instinct made him clasp her tightly against his chest. And when instinct had been replaced by reason, and Romy tried to move away from him, he refused to let her go, his mouth irresistibly drawn to the scented silk of her hair.

'My prayers have just been answered,' he murmured softly against a blonde satin strand.

Mine, too, thought Romy guiltily.

'It's all right,' he murmured soothingly as he felt her heart beat out a loud tattoo which thudded intimately against his own chest. 'They'll come looking for us soon. They're bound to find us.'

But she didn't want them to find them; that was the trouble. She had discovered her own little piece of heaven on earth, as far removed from reality and understanding as heaven itself, and *oh*, nothing could have made Romy stop him from holding her the way he was holding her right then.

'Now, what were we talking about when the lights went out?' he whispered.

Afterwards Romy would attempt to justify what had happened next. She would tell herself that it had been her first close encounter with an experienced man who was able to seduce her with just the right mixture of desire and restraint.

She would also try to convince herself that it had been curiosity. And pre-wedding nerves. She had never kissed another man apart from her fiancé and what harm would one kiss do? A brief moment of madness before the lifelong commitment which was marriage was perfectly natural.

In the strange, private world of the broken-down lift events took on an unreal quality. There in the warm darkness it was all too easy to give in to this elemental desire without any feeling of shame.

'This,' she whispered back, and raised her face to his.

Her mouth tasted of toothpaste, and a faint scent of rain-washed meadows clung to her skin and her hair. To Dominic, she tasted and smelt so *clean* and so pure and so fresh. She was like a long shower at the end of a grimy day's work in the city. A refreshing drink after being parched for so long.

Oh, for heaven's sake, he silently remonstrated with himself. Is it abstinence which is making you so fanciful? Because you haven't had a woman for over a year? But then he felt her lips parting beneath his, and an overwhelming rush of desire made him give a small, tortured moan as he deepened the kiss.

Romy had meant only to kiss him, but a need far stronger than her good intentions soon had her threading her fingers luxuriously through his thick dark hair, gasping with a kind of compliant greed as his fingers drifted over the taut, straining mounds of her breasts.

'You *shouldn't*!' she gasped, the words wrung reluctantly from her lips.

'I know, but you'd kill me if I stopped, wouldn't you?'

Say *no*, said some remote section of her mind which was still thinking logically. Go on, say it...*say* it! 'Yes! Yes! *Yes!* Yes, I would kill you!'

He laughed, but a little unsteadily, as though the strength of her desire had startled him. Her passion seemed so at odds with her blonde, scrubbed innocence. Unless the innocence was a sham, he thought reluctantly...

He let his mouth slowly drift along the gentle curve of her jaw, anointing her with tiny, feather-light kisses which seemed to incite her even more. Her head fell back helplessly, so that her breasts were offered up to his mouth with a kind of wanton abandon.

Romy was on fire as he peeled the T-shirt up her torso until her pert breasts in the lacy bra were revealed. She felt the cool rush of air to her heated skin as he freed the front fastening of the bra and impatiently pushed the filmy fabric aside.

And when he began to suckle her the pleasure was almost as unbearable as the frustration she felt, knowing that she must call a halt to this madness.

In a minute, she promised herself. I'll stop him in a minute.

But he pulled her roughly against him and she felt her body writhing against the hard pressure of his. Frantically, their mouths collided, their kisses fiery and passionate as they both fruitlessly attempted to derive the ultimate satisfaction from kissing alone.

If there had been enough room to turn her over onto her back and take her right there and then, then Dominic suspected that he would have done. As it was, he knew that he must be the one to call a halt to things. And quickly.

He drew a long, shuddering breath. 'If we don't stop,' he warned her huskily, 'you know what's going to happen?'

The sound of his voice should have brought Romy back to her senses, but it did no such thing. She felt as though she had wandered unawares into an enchanted place, which she had no desire to leave.

She ignored his question and instead kissed his neck and the lobe of his ear, over and over again. As she slid her palms down over the hard-packed muscle of his chest she felt him shudder with some unnamed emotion. She heard his helpless groan as he slid his hand all the way up her skirt, and when his fingertip skated lightly over the moist silk of her panties Romy nearly passed out with pleasure.

She heard him utter some terse little exclamation as he felt the tension building in her.

He stilled for a moment, and when he spoke his words seemed to be forced out only with the most intense effort. 'Do you want me to stop?'

She could not see his face, but the softness underlying his words destroyed all the doubts which she was stubbornly refusing to heed anyway. She opened her mouth to speak, but words simply refused to come, and by now her body was starting to react in the most extraordinary way as he began to touch her again.

She felt a hot, trembling ache building up inside her, orchestrated by the expert caress of his finger as it continued to stroke her so intimately—with tantalising little sweeps which took her closer and closer to unimaginable heights. She was poised on the edge of something so beautiful that she hardly dared acknowledge it, for fear that it was all a figment of her fevered imagination.

'Do you?' he repeated, and then again, '*Do* you?' but much more urgently this time.

Stop? The word seeped into her passion-befuddled brain, but barely registered. Through a bone-dry throat, Romy tried and failed to speak. *Stop*? The world would surely cease spinning if he stopped now. She tried to shake her head, but whether or not he observed the movement Romy had no idea, because he seemed to have taken the decision for himself.

The delicate rhythm of his finger quickened and changed. The something too beautiful once again beckoned, only this time it was deliciously close, dangerously close—and as it came into focus Romy clutched his shoulders convulsively, her head falling back.

'Oh, no!' she gasped in disbelief as the waves of pleasure began to engulf her. *'No!'*

He smiled as he saw the tell-tale dilating of her eyes, and watched with rapt interest as her back arched and her limbs froze. He heard her frantic little cry of fulfilment, and a wave of desire so strong that it completely obliterated every sane thought washed over him.

'Was that good?' he whispered against her ear as he tightened his arms possessively around her.

She revelled in the way he tenderly stroked her hair once more as the spasms faded and she somehow found her way back to reality. 'You know it was,' she murmured with sleepy delight.

'So why don't you climb on top now?' he suggested silkily, and Romy's eyes widened as she realised exactly what he wanted her to do.

Quite how she would have answered his sexy proposal Romy never knew, because from somewhere above them came the sound of machinery creaking into life, and anxious voices shouting as the lights blazed unwelcomely down on them.

It was both a highly erotic and extremely damning sight.

Romy was lying sprawled over the floor, her pose one of rapturous abandonment, while the dark-haired man was hurriedly pulling her skirt down over her naked thighs.

Someone shouted again.

Dominic swore in a language that Romy had never heard before.

She sat up. '*What* did you say?' she managed, her voice all slumbrous with the aftermath of passion.

He threw her a rueful glance. 'You wouldn't want to know. I just thoroughly cursed our rescuers.'

'Funny language,' yawned Romy.

'It's Cantonese.' He smiled into her eyes and Romy smiled back—until the meaning of his word hit her like a savage blow to the solar plexus.

'*Cantonese?*' she breathed faintly.

'That's right.' He deftly did up her bra and pulled her T-shirt down to cover it. 'They speak it in—'

'Hong Kong,' Romy supplied in a broken voice as the full, ghastly horror of the truth hit her.

'Yes. How on earth did you...?' He stared, and then his face froze, and Romy could tell the exact moment that the awful truth hit *him*.

'*No!*' he declared savagely, and slammed the door of the lift with the flat of his hand. 'Please tell me it's not true!'

Romy could not do that, but she needed to tell him something else. That whatever had happened to her back then had been way beyond her control. And that she had done something so outrageously out of character that she was at a loss to understand it.

'Please listen. I just want you to—'

But he silenced her with a brutal glare of distaste. 'You are Romy Salisbury and I'm Dominic Dashwood,' he said, in the kind of voice which made him sound as though he was about to be physically sick. 'And tomorrow I'm due to be best man at your wedding to Mark Ackroyd.'

CHAPTER THREE

THE chinking of ice in glasses brought Romy back to the present and it took a moment for the shivering horror of her memories to disappear. Swallowing down the distaste which soured her mouth, she looked up to see Dominic placing a tray of drinks on a small table.

He handed her a frosted glass brimming with juice and subjected her to a brief, hard scrutiny. 'Taking a pleasant trip down memory lane, were you, Romy?' he mocked.

'*Pleasant?*' she retorted, almost choking on her mango juice. 'Are you kidding?'

He sighed. 'So you're one of those people who re-write history to suit themselves, are you?'

'And what's that supposed to mean?'

He sat down in a vast armchair directly opposite her, giving Romy an uninterrupted view of his seemingly endless legs. He treated her to a hatefully smug smile. 'I *assume* that you were remembering our brief encounter?'

Why bother denying it? The rise of colour to her cheeks gave her away in any case. 'And what if I was?'

'Then you surely won't be hypocritical enough to deny that it was pleasurable?'

There was a moment of stunned silence. 'How on

49

earth have you got the gall to *say* that?' Romy demanded, outraged at his persistence in talking about it, and at his own remarkable lack of embarrassment.

'Easy,' he drawled. 'I was there, remember? I held you in my arms, watched you as you moved beneath my fingers—'

'*Don't*! Just *don't*!' Romy slammed her glass down on the table and glowered at him, though her anger made no impression on that infuriatingly detached expression on his face. 'Is this why you wanted to employ me?' she demanded. 'Well, *is* it? So that you could gloat outrageously over a one-off incident—an incident I'd much rather forget?'

'But was it?' he mused, in a voice all the more dangerous because it was deadly soft. 'A one-off?'

All the colour drained from Romy's face and she swallowed down the acrid taste of humiliation. 'Are you really suggesting,' she said heavily, 'that I behave like that all the time?'

'Allowing total strangers free access to your body, you mean?' he clarified insultingly.

It made what had happened seem all the worse when he described it in that brutal way. 'Yes.' She put her hand out to lift the glass of juice, but her fingers were trembling too much so she left it.

'Why wouldn't I believe that?' He raised dark, arrogant brows in query. 'Surely that would be the natural assumption to make? After all, I wouldn't dream of flattering myself by thinking that you would make an exception just for me,' he mused.

'Please don't insult my intelligence with false modesty!' challenged Romy.

'Oh?' He rubbed the faintly blue shadow of his chin thoughtfully. 'Then that *does* rather imply that you *did* make an exception in my case, doesn't it, Romy?'

For a moment, Romy was lost for words. Because what if she admitted that she *had* made an exception in his case? And *had* allowed him intimacies which she had allowed no other man—not even her fiancé— to take? Would that not then beg the question *why*?

And it was the last question she wanted him to ask her—because she didn't have the courage to answer it honestly, not even to herself.

She closed her eyes briefly in an attempt to calm herself—something which was impossible when confronted with that cool silver gaze—and when she opened them again something of her usual resilience had returned.

'Why don't you answer my original question, Dominic?' she said, fixing him firmly with a velvet brown stare. 'And tell me exactly why you want *me*— of all people—to organise your party for you.'

He knitted his fingers together in front of his chest in an attitude of contemplation. 'Because you have a talent.' He laughed as he saw her mouth fall open, but the laugh was cold and cynical. 'Oh, don't worry, Romy! I'm not referring to your tactile and highly responsive nature, but rather to your skills as a party planner. When I asked around for the best person to organise a rather special weekend house party your name came up every time.'

'And that's the only reason you want to employ me, is it?' quizzed Romy. 'Because I happen to be the best at what I do?'

'Why would there be any other reason?' he asked coolly.

'Because I remember the way you looked at me when we were rescued from the lift!' Romy cried, recalling only too well the stinging and cringing shame she had experienced. She would never forget that icy look of disgust he had directed at her. Never—not as long as she lived! 'As though I was the lowest form of life which had just crawled out from underneath the nearest rock!'

'Did I?'

'You know damned well you did! And at the wedding too...afterwards...'

Somehow she had endured his stony stare throughout the entire ceremony and had thought that no worse test could befall her, but she had been wrong.

Outside the church afterwards, in the flurry of confetti and photographers, Dominic had turned to Mark and said casually, 'May I kiss your wife?'

And Romy had watched Mark reply easily, 'Sure—be my guest.'

She had tried to present Dominic with one cool, pale cheek, but he was having none of it. He'd even had the temerity to joke out loud about it!

'Oh, come *on*, Romy,' he had drawled, and she had almost recoiled from the ice-cold accusation in his eyes. 'Surely, as best man, I deserve a proper kiss?'

He had emphasised the word 'deserve' so that it had a double meaning which none of the assembled guests would understand. And in a way that had made things even worse than they already were. The secret little messages which were passing between the two of them had only seemed to add to their conspiracy and collusion.

He had gently pulled her into his arms, had moved the billowing white veil aside and planted a swift kiss directly onto her mouth. To an outsider, it had probably looked like the most innocent peck, but Romy had known differently.

For in that brief, blazing kiss he had somehow managed to convey all the revulsion he clearly felt for her.

And himself.

But what had been even more humiliating was her reaction to his display of distaste. Just the touch of his lips briefly covering her mouth had been enough to start her trembling as she'd recalled exactly what she had allowed him to do to her on the eve of her wedding.

And he had looked deep into her eyes and had known—yes, *known*—that she still wanted him.

Was that why he had brought her here today? To settle an old score? She stared at him now, trying to hide her distraction. 'Do you really expect me to work for you, Dominic? After everything that has happened between us?'

'Are you saying you would find it a problem, then?'

'Are you *mad*? Of course I would find it a problem!'

'Then why are you here?' he questioned coolly. 'You came to be interviewed about taking the job knowing my identity. I know for a fact that you don't need the money—after all, one of the reasons you married Mark was to get your greedy little hands on

his money, wasn't it? So why? Why even consider
it?'

Romy drew a deep breath, deciding to ignore his
unjust accusation about Mark's money. If she denied
it, he wouldn't believe her—so why bother?
Everything Romy owned, she had earned herself. And
as for the question of why she was here, well, that
was a question she could only partly bear to answer.

'Because on the bright, clear landscape of my life,'
she declared passionately, 'you are the only blot on
the horizon!'

Her words didn't cause a flicker of reaction. He
simply continued to subject her to that disturbingly
impartial stare.

'Really? I find that difficult to believe,' he said
softly, then saw her face. 'Oh, don't get me wrong—
I can see exactly why you have such a burning aver-
sion to me and yet at the same time a need to exorcise
me from your memory. But I would have thought that
there was a far bigger blot on your life—a blot, moreover, that is now impossible to erase.'

She knew from his accusing tone exactly what he
meant, but still she had the masochistic need to hear
him say it. 'What are you talking about?'

'I'm talking about *Mark*!' he seethed. 'Mark, the
man you went ahead and cuckolded the day before
you married him! Maybe that, in itself, was under-
standable,' he ground out, 'in someone with a higher
than average libido—which I am assuming you must
have, if satisfaction comes so easily and so bizarrely
to you. But even after having let me touch you in that
way, do all the things I did, you still didn't have the

decency to make what amends you could, did you, Romy? To do the right thing by Mark—'

'And how should I have done the right thing by Mark, Dominic?' Romy questioned, her voice carrying all the emotional range of a robot.

'By damn well *cancelling* the wedding!' he lashed back. 'By telling him you couldn't go through with it! But oh, no, that was out of the question, wasn't it? Romy Salisbury saw marriage to a rich man like Mark as an out—and you wanted out badly, didn't you, sweetheart? So badly that you were prepared to go into marriage with something like that on your conscience!'

'Are you suggesting that I used marriage to Mark as an escape route?'

'What do you think?' came the sardonic retort. 'You were well-known for having a turbulent background. A shallow, promiscuous mother—'

She covered her ears with her hands, but it did no good, for his deep voice penetrated as it continued to denounce her.

'Mounting debts, the threat of eviction...'

'H-how the hell did you find all that out?' demanded Romy in a trembling voice.

His mouth twisted with scorn. 'Facts are easy to establish if you go about it in the right way.'

'Then *why*? What good could it possibly have done you? Why dig into my background?'

'*Why?*' He shot her an incredulous stare. 'Because the whole situation was mad, and I needed to make some sense out of the madness. I needed to know why a young and beautiful girl would, in this day and age, enter into the already precarious institution of marriage when the foundations of your relationship with Mark were about as stable as quicksand. That's *why*, Romy!'

'I see.'

'Do you?' he demanded sarcastically. 'Tell me— are you always so reasonable? Or are there times at the dead of night when the burden of guilt gets too much? When you pace the floor—blaming yourself for Mark's death?'

'Have you quite finished?' she demanded.

'Not really, no.' He gave a low, bitter laugh which made Romy shiver beneath the soft material of her jacket. 'I haven't even started, sweetheart.'

The way his tongue sensually caressed the word 'sweetheart' made Romy begin to tingle with a sexual awareness she had thought long dead. She wasn't sure whether to be relieved or not. Because her sexual response seemed to begin and end with this man, and she needed to find out why. And *that* was one of the reasons why she was here, though she would never dare to tell Dominic so.

And what if, as the sensible half of her was inclined to do, she walked out right now—telling him what he could do with his wretched job? Wouldn't that just leave the whole issue of what had happened between them five years ago completely unresolved?

Was she going to allow herself to be intimidated by him? Or was she going to show him that she had grown up, and that handsome, powerful men could no longer manipulate her? She set her face into a serene mask. 'Hadn't we better discuss this party, instead of our stormy past?'

It gave Romy a tremendous amount of satisfaction just to see the way his eyes narrowed with suspicion.

'You mean—you're still prepared to consider taking the job?'

She gave him a level look. 'Yes—I'm still prepared to consider it. Provided that the house party is genuine, of course.'

Clearly he was not used to having his integrity questioned, for a disbelieving frown furrowed his brow. 'And just what is *that* supposed to mean?' he snarled.

Romy shrugged. 'Well,' she suggested innocently, 'you could easily have manufactured the whole event, now, couldn't you?'

'And why would I do that?' he asked softly.

'So that you would have a legitimate excuse for inviting me here?'

This seemed to amuse him. 'You really rate yourself very highly, don't you, Romy? If you think that a man would go to those lengths just to entice you into his home.'

She supposed that it had been a ridiculously cheeky thing to say. As if a man like Dominic would be bothered to do something like that. 'So the party *is* genuine?'

'Of course it's genuine!' he snapped.

Romy finished off the last of her juice, put the glass down on the table and gave him a steady look. 'Then why did you try to keep your identity hidden from me? You knew I would have to find out sooner or later.'

He smiled then, as roguishly as it was possible to smile, and Romy felt a sudden pang of desire and a rush of adrenalin that made her feel quite dizzy and uncomfortable.

'Perhaps I was worried that you wouldn't take the job,' he murmured. 'And perhaps because surprise is always such an effective tactic...'

'*Tactic*, Dominic?' She emphasised the word archly and threw him a questioning look. 'Talking tactics makes it sound as though we're discussing warfare!'

'Well, aren't we?' he challenged softly.

She stared into stormy eyes that you could lose yourself in quite easily. And thank goodness she was no longer in the market for letting herself do so! 'I don't—know,' she answered rather falteringly. 'I didn't come here looking for confrontation.'

'Then what *did* you come here looking for?'

'I don't have to answer that,' said Romy mulishly. How could she, when she didn't even know the answer herself?

Reluctant amusement lit the depths of his eyes. 'What an obstinate woman you are, Romy Salisbury,' he murmured, with a smile most movie stars would have envied. 'More juice?'

'No, thanks.' She bent down and lifted up the brown leather briefcase which lay at her feet. 'I think we'd better get down to discussing business—see if we can manage to work together.'

'Of course,' he murmured, his mouth curving into a faint smile as he saw the expression of doubt on her face.

He had forgotten just how feisty she could be—but that was hardly surprising. He had probably spent a couple of hours with her at the most, and yet he had been unable to shift the memory which had clung so stubbornly to his mind.

Romy took out a large, leather-bound notebook and fixed him with what she hoped was a cool, efficient look. 'You really ought to outline what you want for your party. You've left this meeting very late, considering that we have just a fortnight to organise it! In fact, if you hadn't made the booking so far in advance, there would have been no chance of getting me.'

'I know.'

So it was no spur-of-the-moment thing. He had planned this. Planned *her*.

Why?

She cocked her head to one side, a heavy strand of blonde hair falling into her eye, and she impatiently brushed it aside as she said briskly, 'I think you'd better provide me with some information.'

'Tell me what you want, sweetheart,' he mocked, 'and I'll give it to you.'

Somehow she managed not to react to the blatantly sexual taunt. 'Like an exact number of guests, their food preferences, some idea of your timetable?'

He glanced down at his wristwatch. 'I'm running awfully short of time, I'm afraid. I'm due at a meeting. Can we arrange another date to discuss the details?'

But Romy was miles away, allowing herself to look at the room properly for the first time, taking in the floaty muslin drapes and the pale furniture and the elegant black sculpture of a giraffe which dominated one corner of the room. It was a highly masculine room, on which he had stamped his own indomitable presence. But, all the same, it remained awfully stark, she decided.

Romy told herself that it was just professional perfectionism which made her long to arrange a huge, fragrant bowl of sweet-peas on top of the grand piano and to stand three simple spears of delphinium in a stark blue vase on the mantelpiece. 'Of course we can,' she answered stiffly. 'When?'

'I can meet you in town, if it's easier,' he suggested, in a manner that might almost have been described as friendly if it had not been for the distinctly hostile glittering in his eyes. 'Say, dinner next Tuesday? You live in Kensington, don't you?'

Romy found that she wasn't even remotely surprised at his offering up this piece of information. 'So you know where I live, too,' she observed wryly. Any minute now, and he would come out with her inside leg measurement! 'You do realise you have me at a disadvantage, Dominic. You seem to know everything there is to know about me, while I know practically nothing about you.'

He held her eyes in a watchful gaze that was profoundly unsettling. 'Let me know what you want to hear, Romy,' he challenged, 'and I'll tell you.'

Romy shook her head and stood up, smoothing her jacket down over her hips. What was the point? The only questions she wanted to ask Dominic Dashwood were of the immature kind to which she suspected she already knew the answers.

Questions like, Did you lose all respect for me that day, Dominic? and, Do all women fall under your spell under similar circumstances, and behave so shockingly?

He got to his feet and walked with her to the door. 'Let me see you out,' he said, and at that moment Romy wished for the impossible. That she could re-write history. That she had met Dominic before she had met Mark. Or that she had never met Dominic at all. Or something.

But hopeless desires weren't going to get her any peace of mind. Only her own determination to exorcise his memory would do that. All she had to decide now was how to go about it!

In silence, they retraced their steps along the echoing marble corridor to the entrance hall.

Outside the sun blazed down on her racy little black car. All around them, the healthy green lawns of summer were as carefully kept as if some dedicated gardener had been up at the crack of dawn, snipping at the blades with a pair of nail scissors.

Up the side of the red-brick house grew delphiniums in every shade of blue—from deepest indigo to palest powder-blue. Riotous pink roses scrambled merrily over a trellis, scenting the air with their sweet perfume as they fought for space. It all looked terribly well-tended and safe and very, very *British*.

Automatically, Romy turned to look up at him to say goodbye, the rather false, social smile she had pinned to her lips dying when she saw the frozen expression which had sculpted his features into a cold, dark mask. Oh, *why*? she thought, with something approaching despair. Why does he still seem more real than anyone else I've ever met?

'And do you like it?' he demanded suddenly.

'Do I like what?' she echoed, lost in the mesmerising silver blaze of his eyes.

His mouth thinned, midway between a frown and a smile. 'The house, Romy—the house.'

People were always asking her opinion about things like that—it came with the job. 'Oh, I like it, all right,' she answered slowly. 'It's just the last kind of place I imagined *you* living in.'

His profile was dark and shadowed against the bleached sapphire of the afternoon sky. 'Oh? And why's that?'

Romy tugged unnecessarily at the hem of her silk T-shirt, so that it showed a pale inch below her jacket. 'It's just that it's all so…so…' Her words tailed off. She was unsure of how to tell him without being offensive. Though, quite honestly, why she should worry about *his* finer feelings when he hadn't given a thought to *hers* she didn't know.

'Mmm?' he prompted silkily, as though her opinion really counted for something. 'So what?'

The word she was searching for came to her in a burst of inspiration. 'So controlled!'

His eyes narrowed, as though her choice of word interested him. 'And I'm not, you mean?'

She stared at him, aware that it was what people always called a loaded question. 'Not in my experience, no.'

And to Romy's astonishment he actually flinched at her words, as though she had struck him. So he's angry, she thought defensively. So what? She'd only been speaking the truth, after all.

'Then I would hate to disappoint you by acting out of character,' he drawled, and put his hands on either side of her waist.

Romy willed herself not to react, and for a good few seconds she actually managed it. But then he dipped his head, so that his mouth was a mere breath away, his eyes dominating her line of vision with their silver fire. And Romy was lost.

'You think I'm so out of control, do you, Romy?' he mused quietly. 'Then let me persuade you to revise your opinion.'

He tantalised her for as long as possible by not touching her, and the fusion of their mouths seemed to take for ever.

Romy shut her eyes fiercely and told herself that she would not stop him kissing her, because that would only make him more determined, but she would not react either.

She kept her lips firmly clamped together, but the feather-light whisper of his tongue put paid to all her good intentions and she found her lips drifting open to welcome him.

It was nothing like the frantic kisses they had shared in the lift—those had been born of desire gone out of control. These kisses were deliberate, and infinitely more subtle—a slow, drugging build-up which promised even more delights to follow.

And if she didn't do something soon she would find

herself in the same compromising position she had been in five years ago. Only this time she would not be able to put the blame on youth and inexperience.

Dragging herself out of the erotic spell he had cast over her, Romy put the palms of her hands against the solid muscle of Dominic's chest and somehow resisted stroking him there.

'Shouldn't you...' She stumbled over the words, drawing in a deep breath to give her strength. 'I mean—didn't you say you had a meeting?'

'I did, and I have,' he replied, his eyes glittering with silver fire. 'Which is either bad or good timing, depending on your point of view.'

'Good, I think,' said Romy calmly, which was a miracle in itself, considering that her pulse was hammering so frantically that she felt as if she might explode any minute!

'So, does my desire make you reconsider accepting the job, Romy?'

She gave him a glacial smile. As if *that* made any difference! This man had given her enough angst to last several lifetimes and still have plenty left over! In fact, she would have gone to a therapist about him years ago—except that she resented the idea of paying thousands of pounds simply to talk about Dominic Dashwood!

And maybe the only cure for getting the man out of her system was to confront him.

Her eyes were as dark as treacle as she drew her shoulders back, like someone squaring up for a fight. 'Back out of the job *now*? You must be kidding!' she told him in a determined voice. 'If you think I scare that easily...'

'Well, maybe *my* desire doesn't frighten you,' he mocked quietly, 'but what about yours for me? Or are you going to play shocked now, and deny that you enjoyed that kiss just as much as I did?'

'On the contrary,' answered Romy coolly. 'You know damned well I enjoyed it! Some people might despair of that fact, but not me, Dominic. Because I don't think that the situation is entirely hopeless, you see.'

He looked bemused. 'You don't?'

'No, indeed. I shall look on my weekend here with you as a kind of saturation therapy.'

He frowned faintly. 'Saturation therapy?'

Romy nodded her blonde head vigorously. 'Yes. You know! Like when people have a phobia about spiders—they are put in a room and exposed to hundreds of the revolting things!'

There was a long and disbelieving pause, and then he actually tipped his dark head back and started laughing. And Romy realised just how dangerous he would be if he ever decided to exercise some of that ravishing charm of his.

Eventually he looked down at her, bemused merriment dancing reluctantly in his eyes. 'And does it work?' he queried gravely. 'This saturation therapy?'

She certainly hoped so; she was banking on it. 'Definitely!'

'Well, it remains to be seen whether *exposure* therapy—' and his mouth twitched '—will be as successful as you think, Romy, but it should be an interesting experiment in any case.'

He opened the car door for her and she levered herself into the low-slung vehicle, thanking her good sense in deciding to wear trousers and not a mini-skirt. But even so he made absolutely no attempt to hide his interested gaze as it slowly travelled up a thigh which was clearly outlined by the delicate material!

His eyes glinted as he bent down to speak to her through the open window. 'Until Tuesday, then,' he murmured. 'Where shall we eat? I know a couple of good restaurants near you—'

'And so do *I*!' she declared indignantly. 'I'm the one who *lives* there! Or do you think that because I'm a woman I'm incapable of doing anything as complicated as lifting the phone and asking to make a reservation?'

'Very well, then. You book it.' He held up his hands in a gesture of terrified mock surrender. 'I bow to feminism and women's liberation and to every other worthy cause you've doubtless embraced during the last five years, Romy!'

She glared at him suspiciously. She had the strongest feeling he was making fun of her. 'Are you what is commonly called a male chauvinist pig, Dominic?' she quizzed sweetly.

His eyes glittered. 'You'll just have to wait and find out, won't you, sweetheart?'

'I'm afraid that I shall be far too busy making sure your guests are happy to pay much attention to *you* and your mannerisms, Dominic!'

He shook his dark head regretfully. 'You speak with such spirit,' he sighed. 'Such a pity we both know that in your case it's all bravado—'

'Meaning *what*?' she demanded shrilly.

He shrugged. 'Meaning that you secretly long to revert to type, don't you, Romy? And swoon in my arms in the most subservient way possible?'

'Are you deliberately coming out with outrageous statements like that in order to get me to flounce out of here without a backward glance?'

He gave her a mystified look. 'Now why would I want to do that?'

'Because you still haven't identified your motives for employing me,' said Romy, and then, seeing him begin to open his mouth, shook her blonde head emphatically. 'And don't give me all that stuff about me being the best for the job—'

'But you are,' he interrupted drawlingly.

'I know I am,' she answered, determined not to show any false modesty. 'But there really isn't that much difference between me and my competitors—not so's you'd notice, anyway.'

'And have you identified your *own* motives for being here?' he parried softly.

'Sure I have.' She smiled. 'Curiosity, mainly. And the desire to get you out of my system.'

'Succinctly put,' he acknowledged wryly. 'And my own sentiments entirely. Though I suspect that our intended methods may differ. Now...' He smiled in a darkly sensual way that had Romy tied up in knots. 'Shall I pick you up around eight on Tuesday?'

'No. I'll ring *you*.' Romy turned on the ignition

with a violent click as she squirmed to try and get rid of the hot, bubbling awareness he always seemed to stir up in her.

'And I'm quite capable of meeting you at the restaurant, you know, Dominic! Gone are the days when women wait at home to be picked up—like a parcel at the post office!' And with that she slammed her foot down on the accelerator harder than she had ever done before.

She dug two little trenches in the gravel as she screeched her way down the drive, but Dominic scarcely noticed. He just stood watching as the little black car disappeared, his face hard and unmoving, a series of dark, unreadable shadows.

He had not been so stimulated by a woman for years—well, for five years, to be exact.

He shifted uncomfortably as he registered the full, throbbing ache of his desire, anticipating that delicious and long-overdue moment when Romy Salisbury would at last lie beneath him, crying out her pleasure...

CHAPTER FOUR

IT WAS only the sight of a police car on the opposite side of the road that made Romy realise how fast she was going as she rocketed out of St Fiacre's gates, and she immediately eased her foot off the accelerator.

Her journey back to London was surprisingly swift, but then it *was* the rush hour and most of the traffic was flowing in the opposite direction.

Within an hour of leaving Dominic, Romy was back in her Kensington mews house, kicking off her shoes with a sigh of relief, glad that she now had the luxury of living on her own since her friend Stephanie had fallen in love and moved in with her boyfriend.

She grabbed a cola from the refrigerator, threw herself down on the large, squashy sofa in the sitting room and sipped thirstily from the can, trying to work out whether or not the meeting with Dominic had done her good.

She had gone over and over her reasons for going there until she was blue in the face.

She had told Dominic that her reasons for accepting the job were curiosity and the desire to get him out of her system, but had that been entirely true? Had her pride perhaps been hoping to demonstrate that she was no longer Little Miss Vulnerable, who allowed herself to be seduced by strangers in broken-down lifts?

She had gone there determined to show him how much she had changed, and in that she had almost succeeded.

Almost.

But what about the woman who had allowed Dominic to kiss her today, and who had failed so spectacularly in her efforts to resist him? Was she really any different from the eager nineteen-year-old he had first encountered all those years ago?

The telephone rang and she snatched it up on the first ring. It was Stephanie, her ex-flatmate.

'Expecting someone, Romy?' She giggled mischievously. 'Surely not DDD?'

'DDD?' asked Romy, confused.

'Dear Dominic Dashwood, of course,' teased Stephanie.

'Dastardly Dominic Dashwood, more like.' Romy scowled.

'How about Devastating Dominic Dashwood?' laughed Stephanie. 'Good grief—I could go on playing this game all evening.'

'Not with me, you couldn't,' said Romy darkly. 'I would have died of boredom long before then.'

'Ooh! Fighting words! Do I take it that your meeting with the man achieved its objective of flushing him out of your system?'

'You make him sound like some sort of toxin,' complained Romy.

'Now she's defending him!' declared Stephanie.

'No, I'm not!'

'So you told him what to do with his house party, right?'

'That would have been highly unprofessional—considering he made the booking months ago,' said Romy frostily. 'I *do* have my reputation to think of, you know!'

'Did he kiss you?'

'None of your business!'

'So he *did*!' squeaked Stephanie delightedly. 'Well, thank heavens for that! I couldn't bear to think of you saving yourself for him since Mark died, if the man didn't even do the decent thing and pounce!'

'I have *not* been saving myself for *anyone*!' said Romy indignantly.

'Sure,' said Stephanie, unconvinced. 'You just get a kick out of turning down every dishy man who asks you out—'

'Steph!' said Romy warningly. 'That's enough!'

'Oh, all *right*!' sighed Stephanie. 'Fancy going out for a drink later to fill me in on all the gory details? How he looked? What he said—?'

'No, I *don't*!' said Romy immediately. 'I've got some stupid tennis party to sort out for tomorrow. I need to write out all the place-names in my best italic writing tonight.'

'Is that the tennis party in Yorkshire?'

'It is,' sighed Romy, thinking of the long drive ahead.

'With a certain young, handsome and extremely eligible earl attending?'

'The very same.' Why was it, Romy wondered

fleetingly, that you never fell for the kind of men you knew you really *should* fall for?

Stephanie clearly felt irritated by Romy's looking such a gift-horse in the mouth, too. 'Well, there's no need to sound as though the three-minute warning has just gone off! This is an *earl* we're talking about here, Romy! He's bloody gorgeous and he fancies you like mad! Couldn't you even show one teensy-weensy bit of interest?'

That was just the trouble; she couldn't. And it drove her mad. She didn't *want* to be fascinated by silver eyes and a dark, obdurate face. 'No,' she said gloomily. 'Not even a teensy bit.'

But then she thought of the forthcoming house party, and saturation therapy and spiders, and the brain which God had given her and which she intended to start using instead of relying so heavily on hormonal influence—which had her simpering helplessly in Dominic's arms!

And Dominic was basically a brute, she told herself firmly. An egotistical, single-minded brute who just happened to be over-endowed with sex appeal.

By the end of the house party, with uninterrupted exposure to his arrogance and his faults for a whole weekend, she should be sick to death of the sight of him...

By the time Tuesday came around, Romy was exhausted.

She had spent a professionally successful weekend which the over-eager attentions of the love-struck earl had only slightly dented. He had just been unable to accept that Romy wasn't interested in him, and that his thousands of acres and family crest did not make the slightest impression on her!

She rang Dominic at his offices, and it took so long for a series of frosty secretaries to connect her that she was in a filthy temper by the time a deep, laconic voice finally said into the receiver, 'Hello, Romy.'

Thank goodness they weren't talking on phones with video screens, thought Romy, her cheeks going pink. Because then he would have been able to witness the depressing little spectacle of her nipples stinging with some horrifying Pavlovian response to the way he said her name.

'I can't believe I'm through to the Great Man at last!' she said sarcastically.

'Had problems, did you?'

'I should say!' answered Romy crossly. 'I had to speak to at least three snotty secretaries who obviously do a bit of moonlighting for the Spanish Inquisition!'

'Which is why,' he explained patiently, as though Romy had an IQ in single figures, 'I offered to ring *you*—'

'Can you still meet me tonight?' Romy interrupted crisply, thinking it would go down well if she sounded both bored and busy.

'Where?'

Romy blinked. 'Wh-where?'

'Well, you *did* say that you'd book.'

'Oh, yes. I have. Of course I have!'

A pause. 'Then where?'

Romy didn't stop to think. 'The Olive Branch,' she said wildly.

Another pause. 'Are you sure?'

'Of course I'm sure!' she lied outrageously. 'Is this the way you usually respond when someone manages to get you a table in London's best restaurant?'

'I shall look forward to it immensely,' came the dry rejoinder. 'What time have you booked the table for?'

The stupidity of what she had done was only just beginning to register and Romy had to think rapidly. Getting a table at The Olive Branch was going to be like procuring a diamond the size of the Koh-i-noor. And the only way she had of increasing her odds was to suggest a time when most normal people had not only eaten their evening meal but were brushing their teeth and about to climb into their pyjamas too!

'Eleven o'clock,' she announced.

'Isn't that a little late?'

Crossing her fingers, Romy said, 'Um—I promised my friend Stephanie that I would go and listen to her sing.'

'So you wanted somewhere near the Royal Opera House?' he guessed.

Actually, Stephanie couldn't hold a tune to save her life, and was the least artistic person Romy knew— but there was no need for Dominic to know that. She *needed* to distract him!

Romy started rustling some papers close to the telephone.

'What was that?' he asked, and Romy could tell he was frowning.

'I've no idea. I'd better go and investigate. I'll see you later, Dominic.'

And she hung up.

'I could hardly find you, stuck away out here,' came the sardonic comment, and Romy didn't need to look up from her mostly gulped down glass of gin and tonic to know who the speaker was.

She looked up to see that he was wearing a suit, and she almost did what he had accused her of longing to do. She almost swooned.

But not quite.

Nonetheless, her outward display of disinterest did not stop her eyes from wandering over him with hypnotic obsession.

The suit was dark grey—a grey that was the stormy colour of his eyes when he was angry. Which seemed to be most of the time when *she* was around! And the suit must have been designed with Dominic in mind, Romy decided, because the trousers made his lean legs look heart-stoppingly long and the superbly cut jacket emphasised his broad shoulders and the narrow indentation of his waist.

'Hi!' she greeted him, rather *too* brightly. 'Do sit down, Dominic. You managed to find it all right, then?'

He was still looking at their table with a disbelieving frown. 'Wouldn't you rather sit in the main part of the restaurant?' he persisted as a waiter emerged through the swing doors and whizzed right past them with two steaming platefuls of pasta balanced precariously on the palm of each hand. 'It looks as though we could spend the evening fielding missiles if we stay here,' he murmured.

Determined to show that she didn't care that the maître d' had seated them in the darkest corner at the back of the restaurant, somewhere in between the kitchens and the lavatories, Romy fixed a wide smile to her mouth. 'Rubbish! Besides, *I* like The Olive Branch for its delicious food, not the fact that half the media people in London are busy filling their faces!'

Dominic took his seat and looked around the restaurant with interest. 'I didn't realise they had an anteroom,' he observed neutrally.

'It is *not* an ante-room!' Romy snapped. 'I just thought you might like a little peace and quiet.'

'I'll certainly get *that*!' he quipped. 'It looks about as popular as a rainstorm on Derby day!'

Fortunately, at that moment the waiter interrupted them with menus and gave Romy a conspiratorial wink. She had virtually had to get down on her hands and knees and beg for a table. Even a table like *this*!

And now she wished that she had not behaved like a madwoman—trying to impress Dominic with her choice of restaurant. She should have taken him to a simple soup and salad bar...

'Just pasta with clams,' Dominic was saying to the waiter. 'No, I won't have a starter, thanks,' he added, in reply to the waiter's question. 'It's a little late for a three-course meal.'

'I—I'll have the same,' Romy spluttered, wondering how he managed to be *quite* so superior.

'And to drink, *signore*?'

'The Bardolino, please.' Dominic smiled and lifted

curved black brows in query. 'Unless you would prefer to choose, Romy?'

He didn't actually say that if her wine choice was as bad as her table choice then it would leave a lot to be desired, but that was clearly what he *meant*, thought Romy furiously. She was half tempted to choose the sweetest, most sickly white wine on the menu but thought better of it. 'Bardolino will be fine,' she said tightly.

A distinctly awkward silence descended on them while the waiter bustled around, substituting spoons and swapping knives around and pouring wine, and then at last they were alone and Romy found that all her bravado had suddenly deserted her.

For the first time in her life she almost wished that she smoked because she was having awful difficulty deciding what to do with her shaking hands.

In the end she knotted them in her lap and smiled at him inanely. 'Have all your guests confirmed?' she babbled. 'Twelve, wasn't it?'

'Ten,' he corrected her, with a frown. He took a sip of his wine and put the glass down, his thick lashes allowing only a glimmer of silver light to shine from his narrowed eyes.

'Pretty small do,' she commented.

'That's right.'

'And the purpose of the party?'

He gave her an ironic look. 'Do all parties have to have a purpose, then? Can't it just be for fun?'

Romy shook her head. 'If it was just for fun you'd organise it yourself. Wouldn't you?'

'I doubt it.' He twirled the stem of his wineglass

between thumb and forefinger. 'The idea of people roaming around my house wanting to be entertained fills me with a certain amount of dread, if you must know.'

'But there's only going to *be* ten people,' she pointed out. 'That's hardly going to fill a stadium!'

'It's quite enough,' he murmured.

'Well, if you dislike it so much, then why are you doing it?'

He surveyed her over the rim of his wineglass and his eyes glinted.

'Don't be so coy, Dominic!' she snapped, when he didn't answer. 'You obviously want to impress someone, don't you? Maybe a woman?'

He met her interested stare with a mocking gaze. 'There's no need to sound so outraged, Romy,' he responded with dry evasion, then smiled and leaned back while the waiter deposited a steaming plate full of clam-studded spaghetti in front of each of them. 'Thanks,' he said.

Suddenly Romy wondered if she needed her head examined. Fancy ordering spaghetti when you were feeling nervous! She could barely hold her fork without her fingers shaking—let alone expertly twist strands of the pasta round it, in the way that Dominic was doing.

She watched a clam disappear down his throat. Lucky old clam, she found herself thinking, and put her fork down.

'Tell me why you're having this party,' she persisted, her fingertips unconsciously roving over her bare neck.

'It's part business, part pleasure,' he told her, laying his fork down on his plate. 'Basically, I want to buy some land in the north-east of England to develop into a massive entertainment complex. I love the area—and people up there certainly know how to enjoy themselves! The land in question belongs to Dolly and Archie Bailey, who are trying to decide whether or not to sell it to me. And they're bringing their son and his wife, too—just to help them decide.'

'And have you offered them a fair price?'

'More than fair,' he answered drily. 'What did you expect?' He shot her a narrow-eyed look. 'On second thoughts, don't answer that.'

'So what's the problem?'

'The problem is that I live in the south of England, and therefore they classify me as a southerner—'

'Which you're not, you mean?'

'I'm nothing but a nomad, sweetheart,' he said flippantly, and delivered the most heartbreaking smile.

The trouble was that the word 'nomad' had all kinds of romantic associations. 'Go on,' said Romy hastily.

'Archie and Dolly have an old-fashioned distrust of southerners, and they don't know me well enough to trust me. Yet. The purpose of this weekend is to show them they can. They're afraid that I just want to make colossal amounts of money without giving much thought to the local people, or to the environment.'

'Which, naturally, you wouldn't *dream* of doing?' she queried caustically.

'Actually, no, I wouldn't,' he answered quietly. 'I find exploitation deeply old-fashioned and deeply offensive. And I feel quite passionate about preserving the environment, if you must know. As for the local people—well, I discovered a long time ago that if you treat the people who work for you fairly, and kindly, then it pays dividends in the end.'

'And does that include me?' Romy challenged, though her heart couldn't help warming to his fervent little speech about preserving the environment. 'Do you promise to treat *me* fairly and kindly?'

Their eyes met in a long look which left Romy feeling faintly unsettled. 'You're the exception to my rule,' he answered obscurely. He finished his pasta, and as he drank a mouthful of the Bardolino he noticed her untouched plate. 'Not hungry?' he queried.

'Starving!' she responded sarcastically. 'Can't you tell?'

'Makes you edgy if you don't eat, you know,' came his unperturbed response.

'No, *you* make me edgy, Dominic!'

'Do I?'

'Yes! So let's just stick to the point, shall we, and start discussing the party?' She leaned across the table towards him and said briskly, 'You need to tell me what meals you require, and when.'

'But I thought that was *your* job?'

Romy thought about it for a moment. 'OK. If you're out to convince a northerner that you're a decent sort then I suggest providing elegant comfort food. Familiar flavours with a different twist. Food that doesn't pretend to be something it isn't—that should be our objective.'

He pushed his plate away and leaned back in the

chair again, surveying her unblinkingly. 'You sound so frighteningly efficient,' he observed coolly. 'You're always talking about motivations and objectives, aren't you, Romy?'

'Well, that's my job.' She shrugged.

'And yet efficiency suggests a certain coldness, doesn't it?' he mused. 'Which makes your oh, so sweet response in the lift that day rather perplexing. Since it doesn't seem to go hand in hand with the very ruthless side of your nature.'

Romy was too shocked to be offended; it was as though he was talking about someone else. 'Ruthless?' she queried incredulously. *Me?*

He gave a cynical laugh. 'God,' he breathed admiringly. 'You do it so well, don't you? The injured tone which sounds so genuinely outraged. And with just the right amount of pouting, wide-eyed innocence, too. As if you were anything other than ruthless, Romy!'

'Then how am I ruthless?' she demanded. 'You can't possibly make claims like that without backing them up. So go on—tell me, Dominic! I may have my faults—who hasn't?—but I've never considered myself ruthless.'

He smiled, but it was the coldest smile that Romy had ever seen. A predator heartlessly regarding its prey might have eyes like that, she thought, with a shiver.

'No?' His laugh was bitter. 'It isn't ruthless, then, to go through with a marriage to a man you don't love? Like you did—to Mark?'

'But I *did* love Mark,' she defended herself staunchly, and bit down on her lip. 'I did!'

'You couldn't have loved him,' he gritted back, not seeming to care about her obvious distress. 'Because if you had, then you could never have let me touch you the way I did!'

She ran a distracted hand through her short blonde hair, as if the movement could come to her rescue and obliterate the past. And make her forget the unbearable pleasure of Dominic's hands moving over her body. His lips on her skin. His breath warm and soft against her mouth. 'Oh, what's the point of discussing it?'

'There's every point!' he snapped back. 'The main one being that although every logical pore in my body recoils from you and everything you stand for there is still a stubborn part of me which drowns in the beauty of those dark, velvety eyes...'

He stared deep into her eyes as he said it, and a shiver of awareness whispered its way down Romy's spine. Oh, why him? she thought despairingly. Why did it have to be *him*?

'Dominic...don't...' she breathed weakly. Don't look at me that way, she said silently.

'Don't what?' he demanded roughly. 'Don't deny that I want you as badly as you still want me?'

'No!' She was about to bury her face in her hands when the waiter appeared, a look of concern on his face as he plonked the next course down on the table in front of them.

'Everything is to your satisfaction, *signorina*?' he asked anxiously.

Of all the words he could have used! Romy nodded and even managed a watery smile. 'I'm fine,' she lied.

'Just tell me,' Dominic whispered harshly, once the waiter had gone, 'why you went through with the wedding.'

She shook her head, fighting down the sudden and inexplicable urge to confide in him. 'I—can't.'

'Didn't it worry you that I might go to Mark and tell him what had happened?'

Her eyes were clear and bright. 'Why didn't you?'

A look of disgust distorted the hard, handsome features. 'Because I felt too appalled. Too ashamed of my own behaviour to be able to confess it to Mark. He had offered me one of the greatest gifts of friendship in asking me to be his best man. What would he have done had he known that if our rescuers had not shown up when they did I would have made love to you properly? And I would. I would have done it to you right there and then in the lift, Romy.'

Romy's cheeks flamed. She doubted whether he had ever spoken quite so crudely to another woman. And the trouble was that she didn't even dare to deny his words, not even to herself. Because she suspected that they were true. Would they have done? Made love in the lift? With the possibility that they could have been discovered at any moment?

'Then, when no word came that the wedding was to be cancelled, I naturally assumed that you had not had the courage to tell Mark either,' he continued inexorably. 'So I thought you wouldn't show up at the church.' He shook his head from side to side, as if the memory still had the power to astound him, even after all this time.

'I couldn't *believe* it when I saw you tripping down the aisle towards us,' he ground out bitterly. 'With that virginal white veil covering your cheating face! It took every effort of will I possessed not to shout the truth to the rafters when the vicar asked if anyone knew of any just impediment why you should not wed—'

'Why didn't you?' she whispered.

He shook his head again and met her eyes with an accusing silver stare. 'God only knows. Because of Mark, I guess. Because I could not bear to inflict such hurt on him.'

Romy felt strangely calm. She was still alive, after all. Still breathing. He had berated her, clearly hated her, and she had let him get it all out of his system. Like removing poison from a festering sore. It was when things were left unsaid that they caused most damage.

And surely if he continued to show how much he despised her then that would kill all her residual feelings for him stone-dead? For surely she couldn't still hanker after a man who thought she was the lowest of the low?

Automatically, even though she had not eaten, she dabbed at the corners of her mouth with the heavy damask napkin and gave him her most professional smile.

'It's getting rather late, Dominic...' Good, Romy, she thought. *Good*! She had used just the right mixture of apology and regret—as she would to any client if the evening was drawing to an end. 'And I think it's time I was going.'

She saw him frown. He had probably been expecting a hysterical little outburst, she decided with a distinct feeling of triumph.

She composed her face into a placid mask. 'It might be best if you could have a list of your guests drawn up and sent over—with any of their known likes and dislikes. Anything I'm not entirely sure about.'

She stood up and prepared to make a dramatic exit. 'I'll pay the bill on my way out.'

'Don't bother. I settled it in advance when I arrived.'

'You shouldn't have done that,' she objected.

'But why wouldn't I? After all, it *was* purely business.' His eyes glittered. 'Wasn't it?'

'Well, it certainly wasn't pleasure!' she snapped back.

He gave a benign smile. 'So you see, Romy, there was really no need to scrimp and only eat pasta. You could have ordered the most expensive thing on the menu and I wouldn't have batted an eyelid!'

Fury bubbled up inside her. So he was accusing her of being *mean* now, was he? She itched to empty the remains of the Bardolino bottle over his head, or to up-end the bread basket all over those thick ebony waves.

'I can assure you that my choice was *not* dictated by economy!' she told him. 'As it happens, I eat so much rich food in the course of my work that I always opt for something plain when I get the opportunity.'

'Just a simple girl at heart?' he mocked.

'Yes. Simply dying to get away from *you*!'

'And at home?' he murmured. 'Does London's finest party planner knock up lots of cosy candlelit suppers for two?'

Well, there was no need to make it sound as though she was running a brothel! 'I hate to disillusion you, Dominic,' she told him drily, 'but I seem to exist on ready-made salads and chocolate mousse, eaten on the run. I'm much too busy for candlelit suppers.'

He gave her a frankly disbelieving smile. 'Except for tonight, of course. And yet you've hardly touched a thing,' he observed, glancing down at her plate.

'No.' Romy gave an exaggerated sigh. 'Unfortunately I had no appetite—but then, that's not really surprising.'

'Oh?'

Her smile was icy. 'You see, Dominic, I really *do* need a stimulating dinner companion in order to eat with any kind of enjoyment—boredom just kills my appetite stone-dead.'

He had risen too, so that now he towered over her, all dark masculine power which stirred some powerful response deep in her body. And there didn't seem to be a damned thing she could do about it!

'Stimulating, you say?' he murmured silkily. 'Well, that's easily remedied. Why don't you come home with me tonight, Romy? And I'll show you that they don't come any more stimulating than me...'

And, even though a million smart comments had sprung to her lips, Romy took the coward's way out.

She fled.

When Romy walked into her flat, it was twenty past midnight and the telephone was ringing. And she knew who it would be even as she picked the receiver up.

'Romy?'

She was right. No one else of her acquaintance had a voice that deep and that sexy.

'Hello, Dominic,' she answered.

'You left in rather a hurry, Romy.'

'Understatement of the year,' she observed sarcastically.

He laughed. 'Some people might have interpreted that as a desire to terminate our agreement.'

'They might,' she agreed crisply.

'And are you going to?'

'No.' Her reply was thoughtful; she knew that if she backed out now the matter of Dominic Dashwood would remain unresolved for the rest of her life.

Maybe Stephanie was right. If she didn't get him out of her system once and for all then maybe she would spend the rest of her life alone. And who in their right mind wanted *that*?

'But I must have your agreement on several issues first.'

'You drive a hard bargain, for someone who is supposed to be the *employee*,' came the dry response.

'It isn't a rigid relationship like that, Dominic,' she corrected him acidly. 'If I'm organising events in *your* home then we need to be flexible about the roles we're each going to be playing.'

'Oh, really? Now that *does* sound interesting,' he murmured.

Romy heard his voice deepen and her skin iced into goosebumps in immediate response. It really was astonishing how your body could betray you, she thought as that familiar stinging pleasure began to tighten her nipples. Why, she was virtually melting just at the sound of his voice!

'As well as being issued with a budget and the guest list I mentioned earlier, I need to know...' Her voice faltered as she wondered if he would choose to misinterpret the question.

'Know what, Romy?' he prompted sardonically.

She chose her words carefully. 'Whether you will have a—a...woman there.'

'A woman? Why, yes!' An undercurrent of mockery coloured his reply. 'There will be five women there, as it happens.'

If Romy had been a tiger, she would have snarled. 'You're *deliberately* misunderstanding my question!'

'Maybe that's because it was such a vague question. So why don't you rephrase it and say what you really mean?'

The words threatened to choke her, but somehow she managed to get them out in as normal a fashion as possible. 'Will your girlfriend be there?' she asked baldly.

There was a significant pause. Then, 'No. No girl-friend,' he murmured, and added hatefully, 'Do you have a special reason for asking, Romy?'

Romy counted to ten. 'Your love-life is of no concern whatsoever to me, Dominic,' she told him loftily. 'It's just that in the past I've discovered that women who are in a relationship with the host find it somewhat intimidating if a party planner comes in and effectively plays the part of hostess. They see it as a sort of usurpation of *their* role.'

'Especially if the party planner has blonde hair and huge brown eyes and the kind of bones a sculptor would drool at the mouth to re-create?' he questioned.

Romy looked at the receiver she was holding in her hand and blinked, as though she couldn't quite believe what she had just heard. 'My looks have nothing to do with it!'

He laughed. 'A rather naïve assumption, if I might say so. But don't worry—there won't be anyone there who will feel in the least bit threatened by you, Romy. Meanwhile, I'll fax over everything you need first thing tomorrow.'

'I presume you've already booked the caterers?' queried Romy.

'I have. They came very highly recommended by Triss Alexander—my next-door-neighbour.'

The name rang a distinct bell. Romy racked her brains and remembered the statuesque redhead who had graced the covers of so many glossy magazines. Though not lately, she realised, wondering why. 'Triss Alexander—the model?' she queried.

'The very same.'

'What's she like?'

'She's lovely.' His voice had softened. 'You'll meet her. She'll be joining us.'

'Oh.' Romy found her heart sinking with an odd kind of disappointment she didn't even dare to analyse. Maybe when he'd said his girlfriend wouldn't be coming what he'd meant was that she wasn't actually his girlfriend *yet*. And Triss Alexander might be an international model, and one of the most beautiful women in the world, but Dominic was *easily* in her league.

'In the meantime, I'll be in Ireland until the Friday of the party,' he was saying. 'I'm flying out tomorrow morning. You can always reach me by phone or fax. Can I leave everything in your capable hands until then?'

'Of course you can,' answered Romy. 'That's what you're paying me for!'

There was an odd pause. 'Until next Friday, then. I won't be back until late afternoon.' There was another pause, even lengthier this time. 'Goodnight, Romy,' he said at last.

'Goodnight, Dominic.'

It was odd how depressing she found it to hear him say goodbye.

With a heavy heart, Romy put the phone down.

CHAPTER FIVE

BY THE Friday of the party, Romy felt far more in control of her emotions.

OK, she reasoned as she drove through the massive gates of St Fiacre's Hill, so she might witness Dominic 'getting off' with Triss Alexander. She might even stumble upon them kissing or—far worse—catch Dominic creeping stealthily out of her bedroom.

But so what?

It might hurt like hell—and Romy was determined to face the fact that it probably *would*—but at least she would be forced to confront it. And she would get over it.

People did.

People had their hearts broken all the time and lived to face another day. People, moreover, who had shared far more than a passionate and illicit encounter in a broken-down lift!

As well as having a set of his housekeys sent over by courier, Dominic had faxed the guest list to her, and she had found it difficult to understand. Or rather she had been unable to work out just *who* was partnering *whom*.

Apart from the Baileys—both senior and junior— no one else seemed to be married. Or, if they were, then the women were all very liberated, since none of them had adopted their husband's surnames.

The party consisted of Dominic, the Baileys senior, the Baileys junior, Lola Hennessy, Geraint Howell-Williams, Cormack Casey and Triss Alexander. Cormack Casey—the scriptwriter—was the only person she had heard of, apart from Triss, and the last person on the list was Romy herself.

So Dominic was including *her* in the guest list, was he? People often did. They seemed to find it socially more acceptable if the party planner was masquerading as a guest, rather than looking like the paid help! And Romy could more than hold her own in any company.

Perhaps she had been expecting Dominic to have her slaving away in the background, wearing an apron and a frilly hat and tripping around with a little tray, serving drinks!

Romy zoomed down the winding drive towards Dominic's house, and when she finally drew up outside the warm, red-brick building she sat there quietly for a moment or two, just breathing in the delicious scents of his summer garden.

Had he lived here long? she wondered.

It was an awfully big house for a single man to own. Even a man who entertained lavishly—which Dominic clearly did not, judging by his conversation in the restaurant. Had he bought it as a prospective family home—and was that where Triss Alexander came in?

Romy watched her knuckles whitening as she clutched the steering wheel like a lifeline, and realised that it was actually *painful* to think of Dominic with another woman. And it was that pain which made her mind up for her.

Because perhaps she *needed* to see Dominic with another woman, if only to make her forget him once and for all.

Romy jumped out of the car and then had to remind herself to move slowly, the way they did in naturally hot countries.

The heatwave had shown no signs of abating, and it was a swelteringly hot day. She was wearing a white linen shift dress which came to halfway down her thighs, but even so she was *still* hot.

She tugged a straw hat down over her head and had just started inspecting the flowerbeds with a view to filling the house with flowers when she heard some-one throatily call, ''Hello!''

Romy looked up, her smile instinctively becoming fixed and forced.

A young woman whose height was almost as ex-ceptional as her bone-structure was walking towards her. She was dressed for tennis in a simple white skirt and T-shirt—worn with the casual air of one who was used to designer gowns but who nevertheless could wear a dress made of sackcloth and *still* look like a million dollars!

Her short red-brown hair held the subtle brightness of autumn leaves, and she gave a wide smile as she sashayed elegantly across the lawn towards Romy, who suddenly felt like a rag-bag in spite of the white linen dress.

The woman held her hand out. 'Hi! You must be

Romy Salisbury, who creates *such* wonderful parties that people talk about them for months afterwards!' she said. 'I'm Triss Alexander.'

'Yes, I know. Hello,' said Romy woodenly. She had met more supermodels than most people, so why did she suddenly feel completely out of her depth? 'I recognised you straight away, of course, but Dominic also mentioned that you were joining his house party.'

'Did he?' Triss asked absently as she bent down to sniff at the centre of a huge yellow rose whose petals were tinged with pink. 'Mmm! What a wonderful scent—I love it!' She straightened up again and gave Romy a quizzical smile. 'So have you got everything organised?'

Was that a command? Romy wondered defensively.

What if—despite her clearing it with Dominic— what if Triss started getting all possessive, playing the heavy-handed-hostess role with a vengeance?

'I think so,' she answered, trying to summon up some of her normal enthusiasm. 'I've spoken to Gilly, the caterer, on the phone, and I'm just about to go inside and see if there are any problems with the menus.'

'Shouldn't think so—I popped in at lunchtime and my nostrils were assailed by the most *dee*-licious smell!' Triss smiled. 'They were baking scones and chocolate cake like it was going out of fashion! I must say I haven't had a proper English tea for ages.'

'Really?' said Romy, aware that her smile was iced with frost. Just who was this beautiful nymph who made so free with Dominic's house? she found herself wondering.

'The Baileys are arriving for dinner tonight, aren't they?' questioned Triss chattily. 'Thank goodness I only have to travel from next door—I probably won't be able to move after all that yummy food!' She drew a slim hand across her forehead. 'Especially in *this* heat! Much more of this sun and I think I'll expire!'

She looked at Romy expectantly, but Romy felt curiously deflated, and in no mood for chatting.

Triss gave her a mildly perplexed look. 'Yes, well...it's been lovely meeting you, Romy. I'd better go now—I have a hungry baby at home to feed.'

Romy very nearly passed out with shock. A *baby*? Surely she and Dominic hadn't had a child together? 'A b-b-baby?' she stammered, aware that her teeth were actually beginning to chatter.

Triss frowned. 'Yes. Simon. He's a poppet. Are you all right, Romy? You've gone awfully pale. Why don't we go inside and I'll fetch you something?'

'N-no!' said Romy, much too forcefully, but she was still reeling from the idea of Dominic being a father.

Triss looked startled. 'Well, if you're sure there isn't anything you need me to do...'

'I can't think of anything just now,' said Romy quickly. Inside she felt sick with the need to know whether or not Dominic was the father of Triss's baby, and yet she couldn't quite decide how to ask her without sounding rude.

She forced herself to flash her friendliest smile at the stunning model. 'Although I haven't really had a chance to discover whether Dominic has any particular likes and dislikes.' She stared at Triss very hard. 'Has he?'

Triss shrugged her narrow shoulders and jiggled her fingers expressively. 'Haven't a clue! You'll have to ask him yourself, won't you? When's he back?'

Romy frowned. 'You mean—you don't know?'

Triss gave her a puzzled look, and then a slow smile of comprehension as the reason for the blonde girl's jumpiness became clear to her at last. 'Oh, I *see*!' She chuckled in delight. 'You think I'm involved with Dominic, right?'

Romy's jaw had dropped so low that she seriously thought she might trip over it. She tried to look as if she didn't care, and failed spectacularly. 'He said you were lovely,' she found herself blurting out. 'And then—when you said about the baby...'

Triss burst out laughing, until she saw the other woman's stricken face and remembered with chilling accuracy just how poisonous and far-reaching the webs of jealousy could be. And how it had almost ruined her own relationship with Cormack. Her wide mouth softened as she looked at Romy's chalk-white face.

'Well, I think *he's* lovely, too. But I'm afraid there isn't a man in the world who could hold a candle to Cormack Casey. *He's* my man,' she told her proudly. 'We're getting married next month!'

'You're engaged to Cormack Casey?' Romy grinned, relief flooding through her veins like an instant pick-me-up. 'You lucky thing! I saw *Time and Tide* and loved it!'

'Wonderful, wasn't it?' Triss said complacently.

'He's just finished another script—in record time—which has come as a massive relief, actually. I think he was seriously worried that domestic bliss might cramp his creativity! But I rather think it's had the opposite effect. I hate to sound smug,' she added serenely, 'but being in love seems to suit my wild Irish rover rather well!'

'That's good,' said Romy, but it was very hard not to feel a little twinge of envy at the woman's happiness.

Triss threw Romy a perceptive look. 'Are you in love with Dominic Dashwood, by any chance?'

Romy's dark brown eyes widened into such huge and horrified saucers that for a moment she looked very like a kitten. 'In *love*?' she squeaked. 'With *Dominic*? Oh, no! Good heavens, no! I hate him!'

A pair of disbelieving hazel eyes were levelled at her. 'Hmm. Hate, you say? Well, in my experience, Romy, a woman who hates a man does not have that kind of dreamy, preoccupied look which is so terribly attractive,' said Triss frankly. 'The kind of look which you have on your face right now.'

Romy shook her head fiercely. 'I have no chance with Dominic. I never did have, not really. And even if I did—I blew it a long time ago.'

'So why are you here?' Triss challenged.

'Because he offered me the job.'

'Oh, come *on*, Romy.' Triss smiled widely. 'Even *I've* heard of you—and Cormack and I live a very quiet life together. Everyone has heard of you. Why, there was even some snippet in the gossip columns that you and a certain prince—'

'And that was a lie!' said Romy immediately.

'Well, maybe it was—but it illustrates the point that you're a woman attractive enough to have members of a royal family sniffing around you! So why take this job, if things are as awful between you and Dominic as you imply? It can't just be for the money. Women in your field, and with your reputation, must turn down twice as many jobs as they accept. Maybe more, I'll wager?'

Romy had been prepared to dislike Triss. She had been convinced that she was Dominic's lover—either current or potential—but had quickly realised that this was not the case. And she might be incredibly beautiful, and have in Cormack Casey a partner who most women would die for, but she also had very kind and sympathetic eyes. And Romy felt as though she just might burst if she didn't talk to someone soon.

'I took the job to try and get him out of my system,' she explained, the words falling out of her mouth in a torrent.

'And do you need to?' quizzed Triss gently. 'Get him out of your system, I mean?'

'Yes, I do—and please don't ask me why, because I couldn't possibly tell you. Not in a million years.' Because, no matter how broad-minded Triss might be, she would be absolutely *horrified* if Romy even hinted about what had happened between her and Dominic five years earlier.

'I won't ask you,' Triss assured her. 'I won't ever discuss it again—unless you want me to, of course. Your secret is safe with me. All I *will* say, though, is that exposing yourself to Dominic Dashwood's charm non-stop for a whole weekend sounds more like a recipe for disaster than a cure for getting him out of your system! Isn't there any chance that the two of you could perhaps...?' Her voice tailed off wistfully.

'*No!*' said Romy, with a fervour which startled her, even more than it seemed to startle Triss. Because she was not going to give herself any false hopes where Dominic Dashwood was concerned—and because she was beginning to recognise that maybe she should not have come at all.

But it was far too late to back out now. And besides, a weekend was only two days. Two days during which she was going to concentrate obsessively on all his *bad* points! And by Sunday teatime she would be heading home to Kensington, secure in the knowledge that she need never see him again.

Romy smiled at Triss, and it was a proper smile this time, a smile that made her dark eyes narrow with humour. 'I came here with an objective in mind,' she told the other woman firmly. 'And I'm going to jolly well make sure that I achieve that objective!'

'I hope you get what you deserve.' Triss smiled back warmly. 'Though it may not be the same as your objective!'

Romy glanced down at her watch in alarm. 'Heck! Look at the time! I've got things to do,' she told Triss apologetically.

'Of course you have!' Triss bent and sniffed at the rose once more before straightening up. 'You know, you really should smile like that more often, Romy— then I can't see *any* man resisting you!'

'It just happens to be unfortunate that Dominic isn't

any man!' Romy shrugged, then laid her hand on Triss's arm impulsively. 'You won't—say anything? Will you?'

'But there's nothing to say,' said Triss, giving Romy a conspiratorial wink. 'Is there? But no, I won't. Not even to Cormack. Not yet. Men can be so obvious sometimes! And I'm afraid that Cormack has become one of those impossible converts. Now that he's a father and a fiancé, he thinks that every man should join him in a similar state of domestic bliss! And God forbid that he should say so to Dominic! Not yet, anyway!' she added. 'I'll see you tonight.'

And, giving Romy her most dazzling smile, she made her way back across the garden towards her own house.

Romy fished around in her handbag for the house-keys Dominic had sent her. But as she reached the door it was pulled open by a woman of about fifty, dressed in a chic navy dress which was obviously a sophisticated kind of uniform.

And she looked far more welcoming than the *last* person who had opened this door for her, thought Romy ruefully as she remembered that dark, indifferent face.

'You must be Ellen March,' said Romy, smiling and holding her hand out immediately. 'Dominic told me that you would be coming over to help. I'm Romy Salisbury.'

'I know you are,' said Ellen cheerfully. 'I work in his executive dining room in London, but I agreed to help out this weekend. I've never seen Dominic so het up before, though. Is it terribly important, do you know?'

'Apparently,' replied Romy, not seeing the point in keeping anything from Ellen—if she was on first-name terms with him then they obviously had a close working relationship! 'He wants to buy some property, but he needs to convince the vendors that he's a good guy who will not exploit the land or the people.'

'No problem for Dominic, then.' Ellen smiled fondly. 'He *is* a good guy. The best, in fact.'

'Really?' Romy's rather disbelieving reply was automatic, because her thoughts were elsewhere. It was all terribly confusing, she thought.

Dominic seemed to inspire an awful lot of affection in the women he was *not* romantically involved with—like Triss and Ellen. So why, in that case, had he never married?

Ellen handed her an envelope. 'Dominic left you this note, by the way—said I was to give it to you when you arrived. You're to sleep in the blue room. I can show you up there now if you like.'

'Thanks,' said Romy as she hitched the strap of her bag over her shoulder and picked up her case. 'I'll quickly unpack, then see what needs doing.'

The blue room was bold and dramatic. Turquoise vied with cobalt walls for attention and should have clashed, but oddly enough did not. The large bed was covered by a throw-over which looked as though it contained the entire spectrum of blues, and the drapes were huge drifts of muslin coloured in a restful shade of pale hyacinth.

Going over to look out of the floor-to-ceiling bal-

conied window, Romy was enchanted to see that even
the flowers directly below her room were blue—delphiniums and cornflowers and deep blue, velvety pan-
sies. Now *that* was colour co-ordination for you! she
thought admiringly.

After Ellen had gone to make some tea, Romy sat
down on the bed and ripped open Dominic's letter. It
began sardonically:

> Please note that I have given you the best room in
> the house. Though you may, of course, disagree
> with me—as you and I seem fated to do, Romy—
> given that the room next door just happens to be
> *mine*!
>
> But do not trouble your innocent little mind over
> this since there is no inter-connecting door, and
> even if there was I would not dream of doing any-
> thing as crass as trying to break into your bedroom
> late at night.
>
> Unless, of course, you invite me to...

It was signed simply 'Dominic'.

Romy disdainfully tore the note into tiny fragments
once she had read this hateful piece of sarcasm, and
let them flutter into the bin. Of all the arrogant, egotistical assumptions, she fumed as she began to unpack.

Did he really think he could just pick up where he
had left off all those years ago? She pulled a face in
the mirror. Because if he did—could she really blame
him?

She hung her clothes up, then went back downstairs, where she introduced herself to Gilly, the caterer. Over a cup of tea, the two of them ate buttered scones and discussed the timing of the meals.

Next Romy found a basket and some secateurs and went out into the garden to pick some flowers to decorate the house. She was just snipping off one of the yellow and pink roses which Triss had admired so much when she heard the sound of footsteps and ice chinking in glasses, and some sixth sense told her that he was back.

She carefully smoothed her face into a neutral expression and turned round to see Dominic carrying a tempting-looking tray of drinks towards her.

Romy willed herself not to react, but it wasn't easy, particularly as he was wearing black jeans which fitted much too snugly around his narrow hips. A white T-shirt emphasised the light tan which made his muscular arms such a flattering colour. If ever he was short of cash, he could, she realised despairingly, make a lucrative career out of being a male stripper!

'Hello, Romy,' he said softly, and his voice had all the sensual throb of a tenor saxophone. 'Do you know it's ninety in the shade? The hottest July since records began. So I've brought you a drink. It's Pimm's—'

'I never drink in the middle of the afternoon,' she told him primly. 'And when did you get back?'

'It's very *weak* Pimm's.' He smiled, ignoring her question completely.

Putting the tray down on the grass, he poured her a glass brimming with mint and cucumber and lemon and ice and held it out towards her. It looked utterly irresistible.

Romy felt a tiny rivulet of sweat trickle its way slowly down the deep valley between her breasts.

'And you *do* look hot,' he murmured.

Romy took the glass he held out to her and gulped half the contents down gratefully.

His grey eyes glinted as he watched her. 'And no wonder you never drink in the afternoon!' he observed drily. 'Because if you put it away at that speed you'll be flat on your back in no time!'

Romy's cheeks flamed furiously at the implication. He had almost had her flat on her back once before—and she had been as sober as a judge! 'Are you trying to score cheap points?' she demanded.

He shook his dark head. 'Actually, no. I came out here to enjoy the day.' He moved out of the direct sun to a spot where the clotted-cream and pink of the honeysuckle grew rampantly over a large arbour which provided a sweetly scented and shady sanctuary. He sank down onto the grass and patted a space beside him. 'Come and sit down over here out of the sun.'

The Pimm's and the blazing sunshine and the sight of that mocking, gorgeous face became all too much for her, and Romy didn't so much join him on the lawn as half stumble towards him and slide down onto the grass beside him—and then wait in half-frozen terror as she realised that what she was most dreading and yet longing for him to do was to put his arms around her and kiss her.

But he merely sipped at his drink. 'Like your room?' he queried.

At least this reminder of his outrageous message renewed Romy's determination to fight him every inch of the way. 'The room is wonderful,' she told him frostily. 'Although the location leaves a lot to be desired. And as for your *note*—'

His eyes shimmered with soft grey light as he glanced at her over the rim of his Pimm's glass. 'You didn't like it?'

'I didn't like your assumption that I would be inviting you to join me!' She bristled indignantly. 'In my *bed*room!'

He surveyed her thoughtfully and was silent for a long, almost peaceful moment. 'You know, Romy, sometimes you do have the most extraordinary knack of sounding like the most pure and unsullied woman…'

Romy only just stopped herself from taking a sip of her drink; she would have choked on it. She put her glass down with an unsteady hand, and her eyes looked as dark as bitter chocolate as they sparked angry fire at him. 'As opposed to a cheap little tart, you mean?'

'Is that what you are, then?' he questioned coolly.

She was about two seconds away from hurling the remainder of her Pimm's at him. 'More to the point,' she accused him, 'that's what you *think* I am, isn't it, Dominic?'

He didn't reply immediately, just pushed a sprig of mint round and round his glass with his finger. One of its leaves was sticking up at right angles, and Romy thought it looked awfully like a miniature green shark swimming around in the Pimm's.

'You didn't really give me much of an opportunity to form a particularly high opinion of you that day, did you?' he said eventually. 'When I started kissing you, I certainly didn't expect the situation to get so completely out of hand in the way that it did.'

Romy felt the acrid taste of shame souring her mouth. She picked up her Pimm's and drank some more. 'And neither did I,' she answered bitterly.

He asked the question which had haunted him ever since. 'Did you…? Do you…?'

She met his gaze fearlessly, surprised at his sudden reluctance to speak. Dominic Dashwood stuck for words? Now *that* was a first! 'Do I what, Dominic?' she asked him crisply.

His mouth twisted into a cruel imitation of a smile. 'Do you respond to all men quite so uninhibitedly?'

It was like a slap to the face. 'You want to know how many millions of men have done what you did to me in the lift that day?' she demanded flippantly, astonished and slightly alarmed by the unexpected whitening of his skin and the flickering of a frantic pulse at his temple.

'Do you want it down to the nearest ten, Dominic?' she taunted. 'Or perhaps you think it's closer to the nearest hundred?'

'Don't!' he grated abrasively, his eyes darkening with disapproval. 'Do you think it's clever to talk that way?'

'Why shouldn't I? It's what you think, isn't it? You think I'm so hot for a man—any man—that I'll just indiscriminately flaunt myself and allow anyone to do what they please, don't you, Dominic?'

'No,' he answered simply. 'In a way it might be easier if I did.'

She narrowed her eyes at him suspiciously. 'And what's that supposed to mean?'

'Just that I've met women who have no respect for themselves, who allow men unlimited access to their bodies.'

Romy felt sick. Because he was describing her, wasn't he?

He shook his head, as though he had read her thoughts. 'But you weren't like that, Romy—'

'I was hardly Miss Goody-Two-Shoes, though, was I?' she interrupted, swallowing down the sour taste of guilt.

'That was the last thing you were,' he agreed drily, a pulse beginning to beat once more at the base of his throat as he remembered with what delicious ease he had seduced her. 'But there was such a sense of wonder in your actions, an uninhibited *elation* when I touched you, that it did bring me to ask myself whether all was as it seemed between you and Mark.'

Romy felt her voice threaten to crack with fear. 'And wh-what do you mean by that?'

'I wondered if perhaps Mark had decided to play the old-fashioned and conventional role of husband-to-be, and had been determined to wait until you were married before he took you to bed. And…' He seemed to be having difficulty choosing his words.

'And what?' Romy prompted, shaking with nerves at his perception.

'Prolonged frustration is no good to anyone, and has a curious way of erupting. Particularly if...' Here he paused and frowned, as if the subject was too indelicate to pursue any further.

'If...?' she put in, even though she knew that he was about to insult her even more. She stared defiantly at that hard, lean face and had visions of raking her fingernails deep into his flesh, leaving her mark on him for ever...

'Particularly if you were the more experienced partner in your relationship with Mark,' he suggested. 'Perhaps you told Mark that you were a virgin—'

'But I wasn't one, naturally?' she quizzed acidly. 'So I'm a liar too, am I, Dominic?'

He shrugged broad shoulders, and beneath the white T-shirt Romy could see the powerful rippling of honed muscle. 'Why not? It isn't the worst type of crime you can commit. Lots of women *do* pretend that they are virgins, even when they aren't. Especially if they are marrying a man like Mark Ackroyd who happens to be a member of the Establishment,' he continued. 'You might have decided that it was in keeping with the type of old, aristocratic family you were marrying into to promote the old-fashioned virtue of virginity.'

'Making me seem more highly prized, I suppose?' she questioned sweetly.

'If you like,' he agreed calmly, either not seeing or just not taking any notice of the growing look of mutiny on her face. 'You might then have found it exceptionally difficult to wait— especially if you had had a fairly active sex-life before meeting Mark.'

Romy couldn't believe she was hearing this! But she wanted him to say it, and to say more—and worse than he had already said, too!

Because the more he talked to her as if she were some little slut, the more easy it would be to accept that nothing was ever going to happen between the two of them.

'So what you're actually saying,' she mused slowly, 'is that you can understand my behaviour a little more now. And that, basically, I happened to be a raving nymphomaniac who wasn't getting enough sex because I was too busy pretending to be a virgin. Is that right?'

'Oh, for God's sake—'

'And life was hell, Dominic!' she declared dramatically, revelling in the shocked fury which was revealing itself all over his arrogant features. 'Sheer hell! Until one day my passion got the better of me. I saw you in the lift and fancied you like mad. When the lift broke down it was as if all my prayers had been answered, and I thought, He'll do.

'I mean—' she shrugged '—I asked myself, Why bother waiting for another whole day, when I'll be legitimately married to Mark? I want this man right now, right here in this lift! And to hell with the lift being mended and members of the general public being able to see what we're doing! And that's when it happened.'

He looked furious—really, really angry. 'Will you shut up?' he snarled.

Romy's brown eyes glittered. 'But why?'

'Because now you *are* talking like a tramp!'

'But that's what happened, isn't it?'

He narrowed his eyes to stare at her so intently that Romy felt her soul almost stripped bare by that hard scrutiny. His grey eyes were hard and cold, like chips of stone. What she would have done to see those eyes warm and loving and responsive for once. She felt her heart lurch, and forced herself to remember that she was still so terribly vulnerable where he was concerned.

'No,' he said suddenly. 'That isn't what happened at all.'

'Well, then, you'd better make your mind up, Dominic!' said Romy impatiently. 'Either I behaved appallingly because I was so hot for you, or...'

Something in his eyes made her words tail off.

'I should have stopped,' he said bitterly, but the silver magnetism of his stare still captured her.

Romy's heart raced like a riderless horse, and some grim, nameless shadowing of his face prompted her to ask, 'So why didn't you?'

'For the same reason that I want to kiss you right now,' he uttered softly. 'Because I couldn't stop myself.'

'Dominic,' she said breathlessly as he took the glass from her bloodless fingers. 'D-don't—'

He laughed then—a laugh so cold and cynical that it chilled Romy to the bone.

A sensible girl would have taken to her heels and run—just as far away from him as it was possible to run.

A sensible girl would not have allowed him to capture her shoulders with two strong hands, would she? And then allowed him to move her very close to him, so that she could feel his breath heating her skin more intensely than the blazing July sunshine?

And a sensible girl would not have raised her mouth with such eagerness, just begging to be kissed.

She heard him groan her name as his mouth covered hers in a kiss which seemed to be half punishment, half pleasure.

And Romy could hold back no longer.

Because she had wanted him to do this again. Ever since she had roared up to his front door in her little black car, and had lifted her eyes to see him standing there, so elegant and so proud and so arrogantly desirable.

With a stifled moan of pleasure, she raised her hands to run them through the silky tangle of his black hair and kissed him with all the pent-up passion of a woman who had lived in a sexual wilderness for the past five years.

Her ardent response seemed to startle him, but only for a moment, and then he kissed her back. And how! Had he been holding back before? she wondered hazily as the wild, sensual promise of his mouth made her press her body even closer.

'Dear God...*Romy*,' he gasped, already sounding as if he was teetering on the very edge of control, and Romy found herself thrilling to that unsteady note in his voice. 'What is it that you *do* to me?'

The same, I guess, as you do to me, she thought hazily as he pushed her down onto the grass and moved his hard, lean body distractedly against hers, awaking in her an instantaneous response as she felt the warm, wet rush of desire.

'Dominic!' she choked helplessly, but what was meant to be a protest came out more as a frantic plea, and this seemed to spur him on.

He started inciting her with movements which mimicked the act of love itself, and Romy found that her hips had become melded to his as her body seemed unable to do anything but follow his lead. She felt his potent arousal against her belly and was aware that her white dress had ridden all the way up her bare brown thighs, and she still didn't care a bit.

Even while he was kissing her Dominic's fingers had begun to draw tiny little circles over the soft cushions of flesh behind her knees. Oh, but he was *good* at that! In fact, he was good at just about everything, thought Romy dreamily.

And only when he had tantalised her to the edge of endurance did he slowly allow his hand to drift upwards, taking for ever to tiptoe onto the exquisitely sensitive flesh of her inner thighs.

Romy's head fell back, so that the kiss was broken, her breath coming in tiny, shallow gasps as she longed for what had happened last time to happen again. Her arms were stretched taut over her head as she lay in the classic pose of capitulation.

He leaned over her, imprisoning her two hands in one of his own, his face dark and unreadable as he continued with his sorcerous touch. But the hectic glittering of his eyes and the heated flare of colour along his high cheekbones made Romy aware that he was just as much in the throes of this wild and inconvenient passion as she was.

Her white linen dress had ridden up almost to her bottom and his dark head was resting on her breast, the tip of his tongue darting out to spear each iron-hard nipple through the coarse material, and he groaned aloud as he let her hands go.

Romy's eyes closed helplessly as his fingers drifted down to stroke the top of her thighs, touching her everywhere except where they both knew she wanted to be touched.

And she suddenly knew that this was not fair. Not any more.

At nineteen she had really not known where all this was leading, but now she did; Dominic had seen to that. Last time it had all been such an appalling mess that she had not given a single thought to how Dominic must have been left feeling. He must have been left feeling high and dry.

Now Romy wanted to turn the tables, by doing to him what he had done so beautifully to her. But her desire to please him was much more than a desire to play fair...

Because she had enough insight into her character to realise that it was also a power-trip, and she *wanted* to experience power over this man. She wanted to see Dominic Dashwood writhing with helpless desire, and *she* wanted to call the shots this time!

With steely resolve she stopped his hand just before it reached the danger area. Romy might not have had very much practical experience of sex, but she knew quite well that there was a point of no return, and if he started stroking her *there* then she was rapidly going to reach it.

'What is it?' he whispered.

'This,' she whispered back. She pushed him back onto the grass and saw his bemused expression change to one of helpless comprehension.

'Romy, sweetheart,' he groaned as she began to unbuckle the belt of his jeans with sultry determination. 'What if someone comes?'

Highly unlikely, Romy decided. And the honeysuckle was as thick as a wall around them. She shot him a narrow-eyed glance which she *hoped* masked her inexperience. 'Wasn't that the general idea?' she murmured teasingly, trying not to look too startled by the rock-hard bulge in his jeans as she carefully slid the zip down over it.

He closed his eyes as her fingers unwittingly brushed him there, and she began to get a good idea of her supremacy over him at that moment. 'Oh, God,' he gasped. 'Romy...'

She didn't attempt to undress him completely; she was too afraid of doing the wrong thing. She just eased his jeans down as far as they would go and then freed him, taking the steely shaft of him in her hand and experimentally running her fingertips up and down the silken length, so that he almost leapt off the grass with pleasure, and a shudder raked its way down his body.

'You're very good at that,' he moaned.

'Good at what? *That?*'

'God, yes!' he groaned. 'That!'

She tried a variation on her gentle stroking movements. 'And that?'

'*Yes!*' he breathed raggedly.

She concentrated on everything she had ever read in every women's magazine article on the subject, taking care to touch him slowly and thoroughly, with delicate fingers whose feather-light touches seemed to be driving him out of his mind.

Secretly she watched him as her fingers moved intimately over him. She saw which particular movement made his pleasure more acute, and as she did that to him all the more she heard his soft moans of delight.

Two flares of colour ran over his sculpted cheekbones and his dark hair was all mussed. And then, as if some sixth sense had warned him that he was being watched, his eyes suddenly snapped open to meet her gaze, rueful for only a second before that helpless look descended on them again.

He opened his mouth to speak, but his voice sounded almost unrecognisable, it was so slurred and heavy. 'Stop it, Romy,' he beseeched her on a ragged whisper. 'Stop it right now, sweetheart, and we'll go upstairs to bed before it's too late.'

But she *wanted* it to be too late!

And, unfairly, she rather resented the way he

seemed to expect her just to march straight upstairs and hop into bed with him!

But of course he expected it! Why wouldn't he? Her behaviour towards him five years ago and again today would have *led* him to expect it. And in a way he was right. They *should* go up to bed.

Because, quite honestly, they were way beyond the age when they should be indulging in heavy petting in the middle of his garden.

But she didn't want to go to bed with him. Or, rather, she *did*, but she wasn't going to allow herself to. She had recognised earlier that she was far too vulnerable where Dominic was concerned to allow him to go all the way. He would have to make do with this instead.

She owed him this, after all. Then they would both be square.

Dominic realised just what she was doing at the same time as he realised that he was too far gone to be able to do anything to stop her.

No woman had done this to him before—*he* liked to be the master, the one who controlled.

That was his last befuddled thought as Romy, inspired by instinct now rather than book-learned knowledge, dipped her head to beneath his belly and took him between her lips.

And Dominic was lost, beautifully and helplessly lost, as his seed spilled into her mouth.

CHAPTER SIX

THERE was silence in the garden for several minutes, although Romy quickly realised that the silence was not complete.

Firstly, there was the sound of Dominic's breathing—ragged and uneven and then gradually approaching something resembling normality.

And her own.

She had grown breathless, too, and that had been why she had quickly rolled away from him, for she had correctly recognised her breathlessness as desire.

And surely giving in to desire would tip the scales in Dominic's favour once more?

'So what was that called?' he asked eventually, his voice still sounding sweetly slurred with passion. 'Revenge for having seduced you with equal ease in the lift that day, perhaps?' he questioned sleepily. 'Though if that's revenge then I'm all in favour!'

His eyes were still closed, and there was a rueful half-smile on his face.

'Revenge?' she queried, trying her hardest to keep her voice calm.

'Mmm. Did you cold-bloodedly decide to do to me what I had done to you?' he murmured, and, turning onto his elbow, he caught her in the dazzling silver blaze of his eyes. 'Was that your own particular power-trip, Romy—to have me helpless beneath those exquisitely skilful hands of yours?'

'There was a bit of that,' she admitted cautiously, because she had not intended to tell him anything. And yet somehow, when he looked at her like that, she found herself wanting to pour her heart out to him.

'I see. And did it turn you on? To watch me peak in the middle of the garden in broad daylight, even though you knew that I had misgivings about it all along?'

Romy hid a smile. 'Then you disguised your misgivings very well.'

He cursed softly beneath his breath. 'Oh, the misgivings disappeared within seconds,' he murmured. 'Couldn't you tell?'

'Then they must have been extremely pathetic misgivings in the first place!' she challenged, delighted when she heard his deep laugh ring out without inhibition.

'Unimportant ones, certainly,' he agreed. He shut his eyes and yawned luxuriously, and Romy blushed a deep pink as she allowed her dark eyes to secretly flick over him, realising with a sense of sudden, rather prudish shock that he was completely at ease with his partially clothed state. He didn't seem at all bothered by the fact that he was lying there with his clothes all in disarray!

But Romy was. Hot and bothered.

She stood up quickly and smoothed her white dress down over her thighs.

'Running away?' he quizzed softly, and she saw that his eyes were not closed at all, but that he was surveying her coolly from between lush black lashes. 'Just when it was beginning to get interesting, too. Shame on you, Romy—we really can't keep on doing this to one another.'

'I know,' she agreed miserably.

Their eyes met in a long, candid stare and Romy realised with a shudder of horror just what sort of dreadful person she had become.

And she knew why, too.

It seemed that all her efforts to change and modify her behaviour had been doomed to failure from the word go—because underneath she was obviously no better than a clone of her shallow and promiscuous mother.

'There is such a thing as *mutual* satisfaction, you know,' he pointed out softly.

'And there is such a thing as no satisfaction at all!' Romy declared irrationally. Because she was damned if she was just going to let him lead her upstairs now, like a lamb to the slaughter.

'So I take it that bed is out of the question?' he drawled as he began unhurriedly to pull his jeans back up.

Unfortunately, Romy did not manage to avert her eyes in time. Instead she found herself unable to look away from him, her gaze drawn hypnotically to the wicked glint in his eyes as he slowly zipped up his jeans, in the most deliberately provocative way possible.

'Bed?' he mouthed at her again, with a lazy smile.

For a moment, Romy could not deny that she was tempted—sorely tempted. And who in their right mind wouldn't have been, when the sight of Dominic sprawled sexily on the grass would have tempted a saint?

'Do you usually proposition women *quite* so blatantly?' she demanded, her cheeks growing even hotter.

'No,' he answered slowly, his eyes never leaving her face. 'But then I have never met a woman who was so refreshingly at ease with her body. Or mine,' he added, with a grin.

'You make the whole thing sound so commonplace and mechanical,' she complained.

He jumped up to tower darkly over her. 'Do I?' he mused. 'Well, it isn't. Certainly not with you, anyway. In fact, my experiences with you to date, Romy, have been the most unpredictable and exciting I have ever encountered.'

She forced herself to push away the sudden glow of pleasure which his words had produced, because he had basically just made her sound as though she was Courtesan of the Year—not paid her a delicate compliment. 'Really?' she questioned moodily.

'Really,' he agreed, with a smile. 'So don't let's spoil it by over-analysing it. Why don't we just go to bed, and let me give you back some of the pleasure which you have just so beautifully bestowed on me?'

'Bed?' she echoed indignantly. 'Are you some kind of sex-maniac?'

For a second he looked perplexed. But then, to her fury, he simply laughed. 'You flatter me, Romy,' he murmured.

'I didn't intend to!' Romy smoothed her dress again

with as much dignity as she could muster. 'I'd better go inside,' she told him. 'There are these flowers to arrange and I want to check on the seating plan for dinner.'

The intrusion of domestic detail finally broke into the afterglow of his orgasm. His lethargy disintegrated and Dominic saw the world shift back into cold, grim focus.

'Romy!' he said harshly, and something in his voice made her stop and stare at him, a question in her eyes. 'Tell me about Mark,' he said suddenly.

Romy looked down and found that her hands were trembling uncontrollably. 'Mark?' she questioned shrilly, unable to believe her ears. '*Mark*? Why do you want to talk about Mark? And why now?'

Because he needed to keep reminding himself of how abominably she had behaved towards her late husband, that was why, Dominic told himself grimly. And because he was in grave danger of forgetting why he had lured her here in the first place.

A distinctly hostile light glittered from his silvery grey eyes. 'Why not? He was once my best friend, after all.'

'"Once" being the operative word,' she agreed caustically, and now it was her turn to see *him* flinch. 'Because after we were married you disappeared abroad and that was it.'

'And how could I face him again, knowing what I had done with you?' he demanded. 'Knowing that I had betrayed him in the most wounding way it is possible to betray someone? *God*, I could hardly bear to look at *myself* in the mirror afterwards—I'm damned sure I couldn't have faced Mark!'

'And because of that, because of the guilt you felt, Mark didn't get to see you before—'

'Before your perfidy drove him to his death?' he queried coldly.

'Mark died of cancer, as well you know,' she defended herself in a low, shaking voice. 'You're surely not going to accuse me of causing *that*?'

'But such illnesses can be brought on by stress, can't they?' he observed cruelly. 'And I really can't think of anything more stressful than living with a woman who strays the way you clearly did. A wife, moreover, whose greatest pleasure in life appears to be having sex in bizarre places!'

Romy hesitated. He was so determined to think badly of her that she doubted he would believe the truth even if she dared tell him. But it was suddenly terribly important to her that she attempted to explain. 'Dominic,' she told him quietly, 'there's a lot you don't understand—'

'The only thing I fail to understand,' he bit back coldly, as if she had not spoken, 'is why an intelligent man like Mark neglected to see through your two-facedness. Tell me, Romy, did you go straight to his arms from mine that day? Or did even *your* conscience get the better of you?'

His grey eyes glittered hectically. 'Did you rush back and take a shower before you saw him again? Washing every inch of your skin obsessively—afraid that the scent of love was lingering on your body like the most cloying perfume?' he challenged coolly.

Romy met the challenge in his eyes without wavering, though she reckoned that few women would have been able to withstand that withering look of contempt.

But wasn't it best to get all these bitter grudges out into the open after so long? Like sores left to fester, perhaps the only way for the two of them to find some kind of peace of mind was to give voice to the unspeakable, and let all the poison come spilling out.

'Yes, I went back to my room and took a shower,' she told him woodenly, remembering the way she had stared at herself in disbelief through the steam-covered mirror, her skin still pink and flushed, her body still trembling with unwilling delight at what he had made happen for her.

'And you don't think that was a sick way to begin a marriage?' he demanded. 'If you were getting up to things like that before the ceremony even took place then what the hell was it like afterwards?' His eyes glittered with stark silver accusation. 'How could you *bear* to live like that, for God's sake, Romy?'

Romy sighed. It wasn't that he wasn't listening; it was that he simply *didn't want to hear*. 'No one really knows what goes on in someone else's marriage,' she said slowly.

His voice was cold and critical. 'And maybe too many people go into marriage with the wrong attitude.'

'Maybe that's why you've never married?' she suggested quietly, acutely aware that she held her breath as she waited for his answer. 'If your expectations are so high.'

He gave a smile laced with cynicism. 'What are you implying, Romy? That no ''modern'' woman could tolerate the thought of living with a man old-fashioned enough to insist on sharing his bed with just one partner?'

'What the hell are you suggesting?'

His mouth twisted with disdain. 'Please don't insult my intelligence by trying to tell me that everything was hunky-dory between the two of you. Particularly given your track record, Romy.'

She read the silent burning question which haunted his silver eyes and knew that however painful it might be she had to try to answer it for him. Though she ran the risk of him not believing her, of course...

'Dominic...' she began hesitantly. 'I was never unfaithful to Mark after we were married.'

'Just lots of times beforehand, huh?' He casually tucked his white T-shirt back into his jeans, and Romy found herself having to suppress a shudder of awareness as she remembered just why he had to do so. And yet now they were standing talking to each other as though nothing had happened!

'Although *technically*, I suppose, you weren't actually unfaithful with *me*, were you?' he ground out. 'Since penetration did not take place. I suppose it's all a question of degree, isn't it, Romy? But I don't think that *I* would be particularly happy if my best man had his hands all over my fiancée's—'

She lifted her hand then and slapped his face. Hard.

And in the rather stunned silence which followed

Romy stared up at him, her breath coming in short, defiant bursts.

With a wry expression on his face Dominic lifted his hand to the dull red mark on his cheek, and began to rub the spot gingerly. 'You little wildcat,' he commented softly, but he sounded more amused than abused.

'You deserved that,' she told him firmly. 'You know you did! Still, I shouldn't have resorted to hitting you, Dominic.'

'Yes, you should.' He shook his head, the remnants of that reluctant smile still lingering around the corners of his mouth. 'You should have done it a lot sooner, Romy. And maybe it's brought me to my senses.'

'What do you mean?'

His face tensed. 'Perhaps it's about time I faced up to the fact that I can't keep blaming you for what happened. That I ought to shoulder an equal share of the responsibility for what went on between us.'

Suddenly he turned away to look into the middle distance, as if he was fascinated by the sight of the sunlight glancing off the lake. When he spoke, his voice was strangely sombre. 'Of course, some people might say that you would be well within your rights to accuse me of having taken advantage of you that day.'

Romy blinked. 'That simply doesn't make sense,' she said.

'Oh? And why not?'

'Because if I was so hot for you, and so sexually frustrated—which was, I think, the suggestion you made earlier—then how on earth could you have taken advantage of me?'

He uttered the words reluctantly, as if every one had been dipped in poison. 'Because you were only nineteen!' he ground out.

Romy frowned. 'Yes, I was nineteen,' she agreed, now feeling rather mystified. 'But that's hardly jail-bait these days, is it?'

His face darkened. 'And I was twenty-six.'

'Well, that doesn't actually put you in the category of ancient seducer either,' observed Romy drily.

She saw the undisguised surprise in his eyes, and was suddenly glad that she had not just taken the easy way out.

Because it would have been so easy to agree with him and tell him that, yes, he *had* taken advantage of her. And maybe if he had suggested it at the time it happened she might have agreed with him.

But she was older now, and hopefully wiser. And she was damned if she was going to come over as a victim!

Everything that had happened between her and Dominic she had *wanted* to happen. And even though part of her had known that it was very wrong that had not stopped her from acting the way she had. Indeed, she doubted whether *anything* could have stopped her...

'Thank you for that,' he said quietly, and he ob-viously spoke from the heart, and Romy suddenly felt as though she was a non-swimmer who had landed in deep, deep waters.

She needed to get away from him. Away from that

speculative silver gaze which reminded her all too poignantly of just how much she still wanted him.

'Good grief!' she exclaimed in mock horror as she looked down at her watch in the kind of exaggerated gesture usually seen on stage. 'The Baileys will be arriving soon,' she babbled. 'And I haven't even arranged these flowers, and I'll have to be there to greet them, and—'

'No, you won't. I'm perfectly capable of doing that myself, Romy. Just check that everything is running smoothly behind the scenes, and then join us for dinner at eight.'

Romy frowned. She had never felt quite so redundant on a job before! She threw him a suspicious look. 'Are you absolutely sure I'm *needed* this weekend, Dominic?'

'Why do you ask?'

'Only ten guests, for a start—'

'You are needed,' he interrupted quietly. 'To put Archie Bailey at his ease and to see that his wife doesn't drink too much whilst ensuring that she does not feel in any way deprived. The two of them bicker about nothing most of the time, and so a spot of light refereeing will also be part of your duties! And you're needed to encourage his son's heavily pregnant and rather shy wife to talk, and not to clam up with embarrassment. You are needed, Romy, because everyone I have ever spoken to about you tells me that you are a genius at handling people.'

Romy blushed scarlet at the unexpected praise. 'Do they?'

'They do. I'm only surprised that you haven't yet

learned how to handle me.' His eyes glimmered with humour when he saw her reaction. 'Perhaps I should rephrase that—'

'I don't think you should even try,' she warned him, and had just bent down to pick up her flower basket when something very solemn in his voice halted her again.

'Romy?'

She straightened up slowly, dreading the question she knew was coming almost as much as she dreaded meeting that piercing silver stare.

'What?'

'Do you regret what happened just now?'

Did she? Romy allowed herself a dizzy snatch of memory. *Regret* it? That was the oddest thing of all— she didn't feel one bit of regret.

Unwilling to meet his eyes, she studied a clutch of cornflowers, trying to think how a woman of the world would respond. She shrugged lightly. 'Regret is such a wasted emotion, I always think.'

'So you're not tempted to leave?'

'I'm very tempted,' she answered honestly. 'But running away at this stage isn't going to help.'

'And is it working?' he asked obscurely.

'What?'

'This saturation therapy you told me about the day you came to the house. Enforced proximity. Is it ridding us of our mutual obsession, do you think?'

She couldn't help the small smile which curved her lips. 'I can't tell. But give me time, Dominic, give me time! The more I get to know you, the easier it will be, I'm sure.'

'I do hope your confidence isn't misplaced,' he warned her silkily.

Her eyes were velvety black in their intensity as she refused to let him outstare her. So did she! 'In the meantime, I think you'd better stay out of my way until dinnertime.'

And then she swept off without giving him a backward glance, carrying her basket of flowers over one arm, wondering if she had dreamt up the sound of his low, mocking laughter.

Back at the house, it was a relief to have something to occupy her mind, and Romy slipped into automatic pilot.

No regrets, she had as good as told him, and as she went from room to room she told herself that she wouldn't even *think* about how shockingly they had behaved back there in broad daylight.

In practice, of course, it was not that simple, and she found her mind going round and round in circles which began and ended with Dominic Dashwood.

She hadn't lied to him. Because, rightly or wrongly, she had adored being able to touch him like that, without inhibition. Had loved feeling him powerless and vulnerable beneath her questing fingers.

So did that mean that she merely felt justified in paying him back in kind? Or that she had finally grown up and was starting to feel at ease with her own sexuality?

Or were her worst dreams going to come true? Romy chewed distractedly on her lip. What if she found herself on the same downward spiral of casual sex which had characterised her mother's life?

But sex didn't seem to interest her, Romy, unless it involved Dominic—so what did *that* tell her?

That she was crazy, that was what!

Forcing herself to concentrate on the task in hand, Romy found vases and grouped all the different blooms she had picked into dramatic, colour co-ordinated arrangements. She also made miniature posies for each guest's place at the table. Afterwards she carefully left them in the pantry, which was cool and dark, in order to keep them as fresh as possible before dinner.

With the help of Ellen, she hunted out all Dominic's finest glass and china and set the dining table as elaborately as possible. Next, she brought out the prettily decorated place-names which she had written out last night, and then checked that the bathrooms had soap and fresh towels, and left chocolates and mineral water in each bedroom.

The smell of freshly picked strawberries greeted her in the kitchen where Gilly, the caterer, was decorating the top of a fluffy white pavlova.

'How's it all going?' asked Romy, peering into a bowl of whipped cream and resisting the urge to take a blob for herself.

'Fine,' smiled Gilly. 'The watercress soup is chilling and I'm just about to make the pastry for the salmon *en croûte*. After that I'm going to decorate the chocolate roulade.'

Romy almost drooled. 'Sounds wonderful! Well, as

you seem to have everything under control, I'm going to go upstairs to get dressed.'

She took more care than usual getting ready for dinner. She normally prided herself on her rush-and-go ability to shower and sling on something to wear in under twelve minutes. Romy liked a natural look.

But tonight was different.

Tonight, she made a feature of her eyes with a coppery shadow which glittered on the lids like bronze frost. Next she dramatically outlined them with kohl pencil, then used far more than her usual lick of mascara. A slick of vampish red lipstick completed the look.

The result was both gratifying and disturbing.

For once she looked her age—and even if she hadn't done then the bronze satin sheath of her evening dress very definitely emphasised the fact that, physically at least, she was now a fully fledged woman, and not the young girl she had been when she had first met Dominic.

Was she imagining things, or had her breasts suddenly become heavier and more curved overnight? she wondered. Had she somehow gained an extra few pounds without trying? Because surely *something* must be responsible for the way the silken fabric clung like a caress to her breasts and hips and bottom like that?

Even her blonde hair, which tonight she had actually bothered to take a hairdrier to, looked paler and fuller—framing her heart-shaped face with feathery little fronds.

And she had to stifle a small gasp as she stood at

last in front of the full-length mirror. Imagine that *she* could look like *that*! Her dark eyes glittered as blackly as jet and her mouth was a wide and sultry scarlet slash.

Did she just want to hold her own against a woman as beautiful as Triss Alexander? she wondered. Or was she deliberately trying to make Dominic desire her even more? And if so—then why?

Brushing aside these uncomfortable questions, Romy slid her feet into the bronze high-heeled shoes which matched her gown.

She made her way down the impressive sweep of the oak-banistered staircase, her heart jumping into her mouth when she saw just who was waiting at the bottom.

Of course, she had seen him formally dressed before; he had looked absolutely wonderful in an elegant grey morning suit at her wedding. She remembered feeling guiltily aware of that fact even as she was saying her vows.

But tonight he was wearing black—a black dinner jacket and trousers and a black bow-tie knotted around his neck. The colour seemed to draw attention to his height and to the impressive breadth of his shoulders, while the beautifully cut trousers outlined the muscular thrust of his thighs. The contrast of a fine white shirt only added to his buccaneer-like appeal, and Romy felt her knees grow weak.

OK, he looks like a dream, she admitted to herself as she tried not to trip down the last few steps. But so what? Those perfect looks conceal a man who may *desire* you but who will never respect you. Never in a million years.

He chose just that moment to look up.

Caught in the cross-fire of that luminous grey stare, Romy realised that he was studying her just as closely, and that a pulse was beating hypnotically at the base of his neck, and she immediately found herself wishing that she hadn't gone to so much trouble with her appearance.

'You look quite—exquisite,' he said eventually.

'Thank you.' Feeling ridiculously nervous, Romy sucked in a deep breath and began looking distractedly around the hall. 'Where *is* everyone?'

'Having drinks. The Baileys junior aren't coming, I'm afraid.'

'Oh?'

'She's feeling tired, and because she's seven months pregnant they've decided to play safe and stay at home.'

'I'll have to alter the table,' said Romy quickly.

'Plenty of time to do that,' he told her. 'I've already spoken to Ellen. Come and have a drink first and meet everyone.'

'O-OK.' Romy cringed inwardly at the way her voice trembled. Why was she suddenly feeling shot with nerves? She had had last-minute cancellations a million times before without panicking. This was supposed to be her *job*, for heaven's sake!

With a rather thoughtful glance at the way she was repeatedly smoothing her dress down over her hips, Dominic gestured towards the sitting room and the two of them walked towards it side by side.

The French windows had been thrown open to the balmy summer evening, and Romy could hear the sound of voices and laughter and ice chinking in glasses.

She walked into the garden, feeling far more sensitive than usual, and the first person she saw was Triss, looking outrageously stunning and wearing a floor-length gown made out of what appeared to be shiny yellow *plastic*, shimmying across the lawn towards them.

'Hello, Dominic. Romy, *hi*.' She smiled and, seeing Romy's hastily disguised expression of amazement, shrugged her bare shoulders with a flirty little wriggle. 'I know, I know! Eye-catching gown, isn't it? The designer sends them over to me from Italy for nothing, and believe it or not they cost an absolute *fortune* in the shops,' she added, with a grin.

'He thinks that Triss is the best advertisement for his clothes that he could have,' came a gravelly Irish voice from behind her, and Romy turned round to see Cormack Casey standing there, a glass of champagne in either hand. 'And he's right, of course.'

Staring up at him, Romy had to gulp back her surprise that in the flesh he was even more captivating than in the rare photos she had seen of him. And she hadn't realised that he was so *tall*! About six feet four, by the look of him!

'Meet my husband-to-be, Cormack Casey—the world's most wonderful scriptwriter,' gurgled Triss. 'This is Romy Salisbury, darling—remember I told you about her? Is that champagne for us?'

'It is indeed.' He smiled, and a look of such love

and longing passed between them that Romy got a very good idea of what a gooseberry might feel like, and was actually glad that Dominic had remained firmly rooted by her side—even if he *had* remained uncharacteristically silent all the while!

'Hello, Romy,' said Cormack, with a crinkly-eyed grin, holding the full glasses aloft as though they were Academy awards. 'I think we'd better skip shaking hands, don't you? I don't think spilt champagne would look at all well over that pretty dress. Here.' He handed her a glass of cold champagne.

'Thanks,' said Romy gratefully, taking a sip of wine and willing her usual self-possession to come back. 'I loved *Time and Tide*—I thought it was the best thing you've ever done!'

'Wait until you see my latest,' he confided, his gorgeous blue eyes crinkling up at the corners. 'I wrote it especially for Triss.'

'Oh, *darling*.' Triss looked deep into his eyes and sighed ecstatically.

'Come over here,' said Dominic, propelling Romy gently by the elbow. 'The Baileys are being given a grand tour by Lola. I'll introduce you to Geraint instead.'

Geraint Howell-Williams was an extremely sexy Welshman who instantly put Romy at ease by saying to Dominic, 'Stop standing there brooding at her side, looking like her satanic guardian, man! Just go and get my wife back before she starts rearranging your kitchen garden before dinner!'

Dominic gave a lazy smile. 'Lola's so good at gardening that I really think I ought to give her a job one of these days,' he commented. 'Excuse me, Romy—I won't be long.'

Again, Romy found herself dazzled by that grey stare. Was he deliberately laying on the charm to-night? she asked herself mulishly. 'Be as long as you like,' she heard herself saying, and was treated to a sardonic sideways glance.

Silently, Geraint and Romy watched Dominic as he walked up the garden, a striking vision in his stark black evening clothes set against the colours of the flowers as they bloomed in the still bright light.

When he had all but disappeared, Romy looked up to find Geraint studying her.

'Have you known Dominic long?' she asked him, feeling flustered.

He threw her a perceptive glance. 'I met him out in Hong Kong.'

'Oh?' Romy felt her cheeks growing pink.

'Mmm. His reputation went before him.' Geraint smiled with recollection. 'He was the archetypal rags to riches success story. Born poor but born brilliant—with a steely determination to succeed which intimidated a lot of people.'

'But not you?'

Geraint shook his head. 'Not me, no. I admire ambition, and I like Dominic. Very much. He doesn't give much away about himself, but beneath that formidable exterior is a man I would trust with my life. A truly good man.' He grinned. 'Plus I owe him a very great debt.'

Romy blinked. 'You do?'

'Sure do. He lent me his house earlier this year,

and that's how I met Lola.' His face momentarily clenched with something akin to pain, and he saw her look of bewilderment. 'But that's another story. Let's just say that, indirectly, Dominic brought Lola and me together, and I can't thank him enough for that.'

The obvious emotion which had deepened Geraint's voice had a sudden and profound effect on Romy, and she began to tremble, as though some unseen presence had iced her skin.

Because she loved Dominic, she realised hopelessly. She loved him in a way he could never love her. Oh, Lord, what had she *done*?

'You like him,' Geraint said abruptly. 'You like him a lot. Don't you?'

Romy found herself blushing again, and despaired. She seemed to have become so transparent recently. All she knew was that she was finding it impossible to disguise her feelings.

She shook her head. 'No. I don't like him at all. Nothing could be further from the truth. We argue most of the time, as it happens.'

'Ah! Then it *must* be serious!' Geraint smiled and took a sip of his drink, then gave her a quick look. 'If you really want to know—Lola and I thought it was absurd for Dominic to book a professional party planner in the first place.'

Romy had had similar thoughts herself. She scooped a peanut out of a bowl and crunched it, more for something to do with her fingers than because she was particularly hungry. 'Oh?'

Geraint smiled, aware that Romy was *trying* to pretend she didn't care. But she did care, he decided suddenly. Of that he was certain.

'It's just that of all the men I know—or indeed that I've ever met—Dominic is the last person to have need of services such as the ones that you provide.'

Romy willed herself not to blush. Not *again*! It was just her guilty conscience which was making Geraint's innocent remark take on a provocative double meaning. 'Oh? And why's that?'

'Just that I could name at least twenty women who would adore to assume your role—and he wouldn't have to pay them either!'

'Oh, I've planned lots of parties for men who are just as eligible as Dominic Dashwood,' said Romy stiffly. 'More so, in fact, since most of *them* didn't have his high-handed way of going about things!'

Geraint smiled. 'OK, point taken. Then let me put it another way. Why hire you for something like this? I mean, it's hardly big-time entertaining, is it? Cormack and Triss and Lola and I are simply friends and neighbours who see Dominic on a fairly frequent basis anyway, while Archie Bailey thinks that our host is the greatest thing since sliced bread.'

Romy shook her head. 'Well, he might think that— but he still needs to be persuaded to sell Dominic some land. *That's* what this party is all about.'

Geraint shrugged. 'If Archie refuses to sell there are a million other, equally profitable sites that Dominic could choose from. So it seems pretty clear to me that your presence here isn't strictly necessary. Which leads me to one conclusion...' His eyes sparkled with mischief, and Romy was intrigued despite herself.

'Oh?'

'That this party is all a huge ruse to lure you here!' He lowered his voice. 'You are obviously the elusive woman whom Dominic has been searching for all his life. And you have obviously played so hard to get—a wise strategy, given Dominic's experience,' he added, with a conspiratorial wink, 'that he has had to invent a reason for bringing you to his house!'

Romy felt as though her stomach had turned to ice. Her? Playing hard to get? With Dominic? It would almost be funny if she stopped to think about it. But she didn't dare stop to think about it.

Because she was only just beginning to realise that her naïve notion of seeing Dominic as much as possible in order to concentrate on all his faults was a flawed and stupid idea.

Because, let's face it, Romy, she told herself gloomily, whatever you discover about him won't matter a bit. The attraction which had overwhelmed her at the age of nineteen was still stubbornly refusing to die.

Could she perhaps plead a sudden and debilitating virus, and make her escape before she got in any deeper than she already was?

'Romy,' said a soft, sweet and instantly familiar voice behind her. Romy whirled round, prepared to offer him her most unfriendly face, and then saw that he was accompanied by a couple who were obviously Mr and Mrs Bailey.

Archie Bailey was a fit-looking sixty-year-old, conventionally attired in a very new-looking black suit, while his wife was resplendent in a floor-length concoction of raspberry-coloured taffeta. Still, she must feel positively underdressed when she looks at Triss, thought Romy with some amusement.

'Where's Lola?' asked Geraint.

'She has insisted on tying back an untidy wisteria,' Dominic grinned, and Romy thought how carefree he could look when he smiled like that. What a pity he didn't do it more often!

'Then I'd better go and find her before she starts pruning your roses too!' Geraint laughed, and set off across the garden.

Dominic turned to Romy. 'I'd like to introduce Archie and Dolly Bailey,' he murmured. 'This is Romy Salisbury.'

Dolly Bailey gave Romy a champagne-fuelled smile, and held out a plump hand which was covered in rings.

'Hello, my love,' she said, beaming, in the broadest northern accent that Romy had ever heard. 'Pleased to meet you! I'm dying to hear all about that foreign royal family—and *especially* about a certain member of it, who I understand was absolutely smitten by you!'   Romy shook her blonde head ruefully, wishing that people wouldn't believe everything they read in the papers! 'There was nothing between us. It was pure invention by newspapers who would like to see him married!'

'And increase their sales, of course,' added Dominic cynically.

'You've been reading too many tabloids again, Dolly!' complained Archie.

'And I shall carry on reading as many as I like!' his wife retorted spiritedly.

'I do hope that your daughter-in-law is feeling better,' ventured Romy.

'Oh, she's nothing but a fusspot!' said Dolly cheerfully. 'First sign of a sniffle and everyone's on full flu alert! And John gives in to her, too! I must say that when I was carrying our three I was out chopping logs for the fire—wasn't I, pet?'

'Aye, you were that,' agreed Archie, with a somewhat grudging note of admiration in his voice.

Romy's eyes met Dominic's in a rare moment of perfect understanding. The Baileys were *exactly* as she had pictured them from his description!

She was just wondering fleetingly how he might describe *her* when she saw Ellen appear on the terrace and glance over in her direction.

Romy put her half-empty champagne glass down on one of the tables. 'Please excuse me,' she murmured, aware of Dominic's eyes on her as she turned towards the house. 'I must go and see to the table.'

Dinner was an odd affair—on the surface everything seemed to go swimmingly, but Romy felt so churned up with nerves that she could barely eat a thing.

She had deliberately put herself as far away from Dominic as possible, but that wasn't far at all, considering there were now only eight of them eating, and it didn't seem to stop her thinking about him for the entire first course. It took every effort of will she possessed not to let her gaze linger on him, and to wonder how he managed to turn eating into a sensual art-form.

Lola, Geraint's wife, was absolutely enchanting, with her wild mahogany curls and her blazing blue eyes. She had recently given up her job as an air stewardess to concentrate on landscape gardening, and she berated Dominic loudly throughout the meal for neglecting his wisteria.

Dominic merely laughed and said, 'Come back when you've finished your landscaping course, Mrs Howell-Williams, and I'll give you a job!'

'You're on!' said Lola, and winked at Romy, who was frankly finding it a little wearing to have to witness all his effortless charm being directed at everyone except *her*!

She drank half a glass of wine and concentrated on chatting to Archie, who began telling her all about his passion for fishing. 'And that's what I plan to do once I'm retired. If Dolly lets me,' he added wistfully.

'I'm sure she will,' said Romy reassuringly.

Everyone had just helped themselves to salmon and potatoes and salad, when Ellen appeared at the door to announce that there was a telephone call for Archie.

Something in her voice made them all grow silent. Archie stood up and left the table immediately, and with one frowning look at Ellen Dominic followed him.

'Probably some crisis at the factory.' Dolly shrugged as she heaped another spoonful of boiled potatoes onto her plate. 'I shall be glad to see the back of the damned place!'

Romy carried on as if nothing had happened, making sure that everyone had enough to eat and drink. Though tonight her job did not seem like work at all. Lola, Geraint, Triss and Cormack really were the most delightful people, who seemed to know each other really well and like each other a lot.

They all led fulfilled and independent lives, and yet St Fiacre's seemed such a happy and thriving *community*. What she would give to live in a community like this, Romy found herself thinking almost wistfully, suddenly aware of how isolated her little mews house was. Oh, it was a very comfortable house— pretty, too—and, situated slap-bang in the middle of London's shops and parks, its location could not be better.

But—and it was a *big* but—her neighbours were practically non-existent. The other houses in the mews had all been bought as investments by foreign bankers. Imagine being able to nip next door to borrow a cup of sugar the way Lola and the others obviously could!

Romy gave herself a little shake. Good grief—next she would be looking into prams and cooing, if she wasn't careful!

When Dominic returned, his face was oddly serious, and he went round the table to lean over Dolly, placing a comforting hand on her plump shoulder.

'Your daughter-in-law has been admitted to hospital,' he told her softly. 'They suspect that she might be about to go into premature labour—'

'Oh, my God!' yelled Dolly, and sent a wineglass

crashing to the floor. 'And after all those things I said about her, too!'

'Try not to distress yourself, Dolly,' he soothed. 'They're going to try to prevent anything happening. But if they can't—well, these days thirty weeks is a viable length of time for a pregnancy.' He squeezed her shoulder. 'She'll be *fine*—I'm sure she will! The doctor sounded very confident. So come on—I'm going to drive you both to the airport.'

'Airport?' screeched Dolly, as if he had suggested drifting to Newcastle on a magic carpet. 'But we travelled down by train! And we've got a hire-car outside—'

'And I'm going to drive it for you—Archie's feeling a little shaken up,' explained Dominic slowly.

'But what about our return ticket?' asked Dolly, her voice rising hysterically. 'We can't fly to Newcastle—it isn't far enough!'

'Don't worry; I've arranged everything. Let's go and fetch your things,' said Dominic calmly. 'Archie's on the phone to your son at the moment. When he's finished we can get going. Romy, can—?'

'I can sort everything out at this end,' said Romy instantly, and he flashed her a grateful smile.

But once Dominic and Dolly had gone nobody had much appetite left. Romy picked up the shards of shattered wineglass while the other four sat disconsolately poking their spoons into untouched portions of chocolate roulade and strawberry pavlova.

Eventually Geraint put his spoon down with a sigh and said, 'I don't know about anyone else, but I think brandy is called for rather than pudding.'

'Good thinking,' said Cormack, but his voice sounded rather heavy as he looked across the table at Triss.

She gave an apologetic smile. 'A quick brandy would be wonderful, but then would you mind if I went home? I just sort of want to check on Simon. He's been teething, and grizzly, and if he wakes up and finds just the babysitter there...'

'No one minds, Triss darling,' said Cormack softly. 'I'll come with you.'

'I hope she'll be OK,' said Lola suddenly, her blue eyes clouding over. 'And the baby.'

Geraint stood up and went to the sideboard where he collected brandy and glasses and brought them back to the table. 'She'll be fine,' he said, pouring them all a huge measure. 'They can save babies who are no bigger than a bag of sugar these days—which will make a seven-monther seem positively obese!'

They all drank brandy, and then strong black coffee, but the party mood was broken, and Romy wasn't surprised when they all stood up to leave.

'Thank Dominic for us,' said Geraint as he bent and kissed her lightly on both cheeks.

'I will,' said Romy.

'And be sure to come and look round the garden first thing,' Lola dimpled.

'I'd love to,' promised Romy, hastily quashing the thought that she might not be here tomorrow...

But once they had gone, and she had helped clear up and then sent Ellen and Gilly home, she still felt in a dilemma, not knowing whether she should stay or go. Whilst instinct told her that leaving was the wiser option, her soft heart remembered the dark, sombre look on Dominic's face, and urged her to wait for him.

She wandered around the house like a ghost, until she eventually found a small study which was lined with books from floor to ceiling. She was just looking with interest through one of the shelves when she heard the sound of a car engine, and then the front door slamming.

There was a brief silence, and then footsteps began walking slowly but inexorably towards the study.

Romy looked up as Dominic entered the small room, her heart in her mouth as she searched his face for news.

CHAPTER SEVEN

'WHAT'S happened?' Romy uttered a silent prayer as she asked the question.

Dominic smiled. 'We rang the hospital from the airport on my mobile. She's stable and settled—and at the moment she's hanging onto the baby. They are cautiously optimistic.'

'That's wonderful.'

'Yes.' He threw her a narrow-eyed look. 'So are you. Archie liked you very much.'

'Did he?'

'Mmm. And he's decided to sell me the land I want. He told me in the car. He grew quite sentimental about the fact that I had interrupted a dinner party in order to drive him and Dolly to the airport. That seemed to make his mind up. He appears to have lost some of his prejudices about southerners along the way!'

Romy smiled. 'Geraint told me that if this particular deal fell through then there were loads of other places you could buy in the north of England.'

'Did he? He's right, in a way. But that land means more to me than any other.'

'Because...?'

There was a pause. 'Because I spent the first twelve years of my life near there, I guess. My mother brought me up there on her own, before moving down here.'

Romy tipped her blonde head to one side. 'So you're not a southerner at all?' She remembered asking him this question once before, in the restaurant, and he had avoided answering with spectacular charm.

His grey eyes glimmered, as if he was recalling his evasiveness, too. 'No, I'm not.'

'But you sound so...'

'I know I do.' His reply was dry. 'I learnt very early on that internationally successful businessmen do not have broad Geordie accents! Oxford ironed most of it out for me.'

'But surely if Archie had known *that*—?'

'Then he would have decided to sell me the land, anyway?'

'Well—yes.'

He smiled. 'He might have done.'

'So why on earth didn't you tell him?'

He smiled again. 'Because I wanted him to be swayed by my sound business proposition, and not by sentiment.'

'Even though he *was*?' she queried. 'Swayed by sentiment, I mean. Having fixed ideas about people who are born in the south. Why didn't you just play him at his own game, Dominic?'

His eyes narrowed thoughtfully. 'Because it isn't the modern way, is it? To be sentimental.'

'No,' she conceded, and a wave of dejection suddenly washed over her. She hastily changed the subject. 'So this land that you're buying—it has lots of potential, does it?'

'I don't know if that's the ideal way to describe it.' His laugh was tinged with cynicism. 'Run-down factories and vast areas of wasteland—that's all it consists of. It was a bleak, soulless place then, and it's not very much better now—though it has one thing going for it in these overcrowded urban times. It has plenty of space.'

'So why on earth do you want to buy it?'

His grey eyes looked almost dreamy. 'Because I always knew I was lucky.' He must have seen the surprise on her face for he nodded sagely. 'Oh, yes— I count myself lucky, Romy, because at least I knew I had it in me to escape the poverty trap I was born into. Others weren't so fortunate.'

His mouth took on a sort of grim, determined line. 'I vowed that one day I would put something back there. Something that others, not so blessed as me, could enjoy for a while to forget their problems...'

Romy let her gaze fall to her lap, reluctant to look him in the eye. He had grown up poor and illegitimate, and yet he could say that he was blessed... Suddenly he made her feel terribly, terribly humble.

Over the years, Romy had accredited Dominic with many attributes—overt sex appeal and the ability to make lots of money being the predominant ones. But she had never realised that at heart he was such a *good* man. Geraint was right.

She stiffened suddenly as she became aware of the natural progression of her thoughts. Because being a good man did not exclude him from having sex without any commitment, did it?

He shot her a narrow-eyed glance, as if he had

sensed her sudden discomfiture. 'I could use a brandy.'

So could she. But...

'I was thinking of going,' she confessed bluntly. 'Home.'

He did not look remotely surprised. 'No doubt you were, Romy, but I'm not going to let you.'

'So it's cave-man tactics now, is it?' she mocked.

He gave a glimmer of a smile. 'It can always be arranged, sweetheart, if that is—as I suspect—what turns you on.'

'Stop it!'

But now he was walking towards her, until he was only a warm breath away, and Romy found herself holding her own breath, alternately dreading and longing for him to do something outrageously demonstrative.

Like throwing her down onto the carpet and making love to her properly, perhaps...?

'You look extremely hot,' he observed wryly. 'Come on.' And he took her firmly by the hand.

'Where do you think you're taking me?' she heard herself squeaking.

Dominic frowned, and then sighed. 'I'm afraid you can't possibly play the helpless heroine now, Romy. Not when you gave me possibly one of the most erotic encounters of my life in the garden this afternoon. I'm taking you to the sitting room so that we can sit down together and have—'

'Let me *guess*!' she interjected sourly.

'A long-overdue talk,' he finished reprovingly.

Well, she had never heard it called *that* before, but

she let him lead her into the sitting room anyway, and then sat on the blue velvet sofa with her legs tucked up beneath her while he busied himself with pouring them a drink. Then he came and positioned himself next to her.

Romy accepted her brandy with shaky fingers but took only a tiny sip before putting the glass down on one of the small tables. As a delaying tactic, she fussed around with the skirt of her dress and pleated some of the cinnamon-coloured satin between her fingers, then at last looked into his face with clear brown eyes. 'So what do you want to talk about, Dominic?'

His mouth twisted into a sardonic smile. 'Shall I give you a whole list of points up for discussion?'

'That much, huh?' Romy attempted to make a joke of it, but her voice stupidly began to wobble, and then she became afraid that she might commit the ultimate sin of bursting into tears.

'What's the matter?' He frowned.

'I don't *know*!' That was the trouble.

She tried turning her head away, but he wouldn't let her, cupping her chin firmly in his strong hand, and Romy almost melted.

He felt her shudder. 'Maybe now is not the time for talking,' he said thickly, and moved his face towards her. 'Maybe we should use our time more usefully—what do you say, Romy?'

She said nothing, for she felt weak and powerless and totally without fight. Her resistance to him had been vanishing ever since she had first set foot in his home, and now it had almost completely disappeared.

Her face was white, her eyes huge and dark and

haunted, and Dominic's jaw tightened. Damn! He could not possibly make love to her now. Not while she was looking at him with all the pain of a wounded deer.

'Tell me about your marriage,' he said suddenly.

It was as though he had woken her up from a coma. Romy blinked in astonishment that he should have asked her such a thing, and at such a time.

But, if she searched truthfully in her heart, would there ever be a time to discuss Mark without all the guilt and regret which inevitably accompanied it?

She sat up straight, moving slightly away from him, and her hand groped out for her brandy glass. 'What do you want to know about my marriage?' she asked, unable to keep the bleakness from her voice.

Dominic hardened his heart, refusing to let her fragile face deflect him. 'Was it happy?'

'No.' She saw the bitter accusation in his eyes and flinched. 'Not in the conventional sense, anyway.'

'Because of your cheating?'

'Because of Mark's illness,' she told him, and now it was *his* turn to flinch. 'That cast an inevitable shadow over our relationship—but we made the best of what we had.'

There was a silence while he digested this. 'And was he brave?'

Romy nodded. 'Sometimes he could be remarkably brave—and at other times he was terribly, terribly frightened.' She gave him a steady stare. 'There isn't a stereotypical way that people behave when they know they're dying, Dominic—there are no rules or guidelines to follow. It's erratic. Unpredictable. It's like all human behaviour—you make most of it up as you go along.'

'And could you bear to look him in the eye?' he demanded fiercely. 'After what you had done to him?'

'Yes, I could.' A muscle worked in her cheek. 'Because his mother had been put in a nursing home and I was all he had left,' she answered simply. And then, because she thought that Dominic was very successfully avoiding facing up to *his* share of the blame, she added, 'And because—unlike you, Dominic—I could not face running away.'

'I did *not* run away!' he gritted.

'You never saw him once—not *once*—after the wedding!' she accused him. 'You didn't even come to the funeral, for God's sake!'

'How could I?' he grated angrily. 'How could I face him, knowing what I had done to his wife? And how could I face *you*, Romy, when I knew that all I still wanted to do was to drag you off to the nearest bed and—?'

'Th-that's enough,' she told him shakily.

'Turning up at your wedding was a mistake, but one that I could not possibly avoid without a huge scene. But I knew that I could not willingly face the two of you again.' Dominic briefly shut his eyes. 'And then, when I discovered how sick he was...'

'Well?' Her voice was brittle. 'Why didn't you come *then*?'

'I couldn't do that either,' he said simply. 'How could I? By then I hadn't been in contact with Mark for so long that it would have been impossible to justify my absence without telling him the truth. And I owed Mark nothing less than the truth,' he finished, on a sombre note.

Oh, the irony of it all! Romy took another sip of brandy. 'He wouldn't have wanted you to come if your only reason for doing so was pity.'

'I know that.' He drained his glass and put it down, then fixed her with a dazzling grey stare. 'So what now, Romy—what do we do next?'

She was terrified that she would read much, much more into his question than he intended, and so she neatly turned it around. 'That depends.'

'On?'

'On what *you* want to do.'

'I think you already know the answer to that,' he said huskily.

'And on what *I* want to do,' she added firmly.

'And do our wishes match, Romy?' he queried softly.

She studied the palm of her hand for a moment before looking up. 'You mean—do I want to go to bed with you?'

He looked slightly taken aback. 'Well, yes...'

'What's the matter, Dominic?' she quizzed provocatively. 'Not used to your women being honest about their needs?'

He laughed, but the laugh was tinged with a raw kind of hunger which set Romy's veins tingling. 'Are you one of my women, then, Romy?'

It was just unfortunate that he had chosen to phrase it that way. Or perhaps not. Perhaps it was the best thing he could have said. Because making her sound like one of a vast harem had killed any romantic hopes she might have been harbouring in one fell swoop.

Had he seen the doubt and the weary resignation which had momentarily clouded her features? Was that why his mouth hardened into a bitter line as he said 'Obviously not'? His voice had hardened, too. 'I think you'd better tell me where *you* want to go from here, don't you, Romy?'

Romy gave him a wide-eyed look. 'Why, to bed, of course!'

Dominic looked at her with a positively *shocked* expression on his face, and it took him a moment or two to recover himself. 'To bed?' he queried, as if he had not heard her correctly.

Her heart and her body were crying out for him, but she managed to conceal her true feelings with what she judged to be just the right kind of modern approach.

'Of course,' she whispered softly, noticing now how his eyes were drawn hypnotically to the pert thrust of her breasts against the copper satin of her dress. 'We can't go on the way we have been, Dominic. I hate to be thought of as a tease—and so, I'm sure, do you. And we've been teasing one another for five long years now. Don't you think it's time we did something to put each other out of our misery?'

Dominic swallowed as he fought to retain some sort of hold on reality. 'Is this your famous saturation therapy?' he questioned unsteadily. 'Is this the ultimate method for getting me out of your system?'

She didn't answer that, just leaned across and ran a finger delicately down the side of his face, and then let it trace the full outline of his mouth. She saw his lips tremble at exactly the same moment as his eyes darkened, and felt a great rush of delight as she realised that—sexually, at least—she had as much power over him as he had over her.

And in order to control that power, in order not to give way to foolish thoughts of love, she needed to be strong.

She prayed for the courage to ask her next question just as he lifted her hand to his mouth, to cover the palm with tiny kisses.

'Dominic?'

'Mmm?' His eyes were closed, his voice sounded dreamy.

'Why exactly did you invite me here this week-end?'

His eyelids flew open, his expression suddenly wary.

Romy shook her head impatiently. 'And don't give me any of that "you were the best person for the job" rubbish. There are lots of other people who would have done as well; you know that and I know that.'

'My answer is clearly redundant,' came his dry response. 'Since you've obviously made up your mind already. What have you decided, Romy—that I brought you here to seduce you into submission?'

'To make me fall in love with you?' she suggested.

His eyes narrowed. 'That's a fairly hefty accusation.'

'I know.'

'And why would I want to do something like that?'

Why indeed? When Dominic fell in love and married, it would not be to a woman who behaved in the way that she had behaved. She voiced her greatest fear. 'Probably so that you could give me the push in the most horrible way possible and break my heart into the bargain!' she accused wildly.

That watchful expression had crept over his face again. 'Well, there isn't much chance of that happening, is there, Romy? Since you haven't fallen in love with me.' His lashes shadowed his silver eyes. 'Have you?'

Romy decided that a lie was acceptable if it enabled her to preserve her sanity. 'Of course not!' she scoffed.

'Well, then, subject closed.' He lay back on the sofa and frowned. 'So I suppose that means bed *is* out of the question?'

'Yes,' she said demurely. 'It is now. Sorry.' She treasured his stricken look for a moment, before deciding to put him out of his misery.

She climbed across the sofa towards him, hitching her long satin dress up as she did so, and she saw the involuntary flicker of a muscle working in his cheek. She would leave long before he could kick her out, she decided—and in the meantime she would give him a night he would never forget.

'No bed, but there's always the sofa,' she explained softly.

His eyes narrowed in comprehension just as her mouth swooped down on his. And he groaned and brought her hard against his chest, deepening the kiss with such mastery that Romy almost passed out with pleasure.

Dominic felt so hot for her that he could barely think. All he did know was that if Romy carried on writhing around on his lap wearing that outrageously clinging dress, then things were going to get rapidly out of control.

And he *needed* to be in control as never before in his life. Because up until now his whole relationship with Romy had been characterised by a complete *lack* of control.

Somehow he managed to free himself from the delicious honeyed softness of her mouth, and she gave an indistinct little moan of protest.

'Wh-what are you doing?' she questioned, quashing down the fear that he now despised her so much, he couldn't even bring himself to make love to her.

Dominic rose to his feet, his arm around her bare back so that she came with him. 'I'm taking you upstairs, Romy. To my bedroom. Where I can slowly peel every article of clothing from that delicious body of yours. Then I'm going to lay you down between sheets of the finest white linen and make love to you over and over again until I've filled you so completely that you beg me to stop.'

Romy shuddered.

'Yes,' he breathed. 'I can see your body trembling in anticipation, just like mine is trembling now, with pure, sweet desire. See, sweetheart.' And to demonstrate he held both his hands up towards her and Romy saw that yes, indeed, they were shaking like mad.

But what he didn't realise was that she was trembling with fear, a fear which had completely swamped her desire. She absolutely *dreaded* seeing his bed— the scene, no doubt, of countless other seductions.

And she dreaded the inevitable comparisons. She was *bound* to fare badly in the good-in-bed stakes— especially when measured up against some of the experienced beauties who had cavorted all over the place with him.

He must have felt her stiffen, for he lifted her chin and looked down into her face, his stern expression giving way to something almost approaching disappointment as he read her sudden withdrawal.

'Just what *is* it with you?' he demanded, in a voice which rang with an odd, cold kind of exasperation. 'Don't you get turned on by straight sex any more, Romy? Is your appetite so jaded that you can only get your kicks in the most bizarre ways possible? In the lift? In the garden? And now you want us to make love for the first time on the sofa—as if we were two teenagers with nowhere to go!'

'Don't!' she told him tightly. 'Please don't.'

'But why not?' he queried, in mock surprise. 'I'm interested to hear what you have to say. Isn't there a name for people who like making love in public places? Is that what turns you on, Romy—the fear of discovery? Does it enhance your pleasure to think that someone might stumble in on us just as you're helplessly gasping out at the height of your orgasm? Does it?'

The trouble was that his words—far from appalling her—were actually turning her on to a pitch that was becoming impossible to conceal.

And Dominic noticed, too—for he gave a cynical

little laugh as his eyes raked over her. He saw the blatant tightening of her nipples, outlined starkly against the rich satin of her bodice. He noticed the distracted little way she circled her hips, the way her breath came in short, shallow gasps. Her eyes looked as black as hell, and he would have bet his entire fortune that if he'd snaked one of his hands all the way up her leg to her panties she would have practically begged him to remove them.

He pushed her back onto the sofa, his eyes glittering wildly. 'So this is how you like it, is it? Hmm? And what next? Tell me what you like best, Romy, and I'll do it to you.' His eyes narrowed as she made no response.

'Let me guess,' he continued inexorably. 'You want it hard and you want it fast, right? You want me to rip your panties off and just thrust straight into you, don't you, sweetheart? Because that's how you like it! Greedy and rapacious—that's what turns you on most. And, like all sexually greedy people, it's instant gratification that you crave. The instant buzz. The quick fix. Like a take-away meal, you simply want sex to satisfy your hunger. Don't you, Romy?'

How she longed to slap his horrible, arrogant face and push him away. But she couldn't. *Couldn't.* His words were driving her absolutely mad with desire.

'I—' Romy sucked breath desperately into her lungs, so on fire with arousal that she could not speak. Her head flopped helplessly back against the cushions of the sofa, and her eyelids fluttered to a close.

'Oh, it's like that, is it?' he queried softly as he saw her wriggle her hips distractedly. 'You really *do* want me badly, don't you, Romy? I think you want me to do…this…'

Romy let out a tortured little cry as his finger alighted on the slippery surface of her bodice and almost negligently traced a line around the swollen mound of her breast.

'Yes, you like that, don't you?' he mused.

His finger traced feather-light little circles, and Romy almost sobbed with frustration.

'Yes,' he said, in a deep, satisfied voice. 'I know what you like best, Romy, but you're not going to get it.'

Romy's eyes flew open in genuine alarm. 'I'm n-not?' She stumbled over the words.

He smiled, but Romy thought how dark and how cruel his eyes looked. 'No, indeed. I'm going to show you that making love can be a long, slow feast which works far more keenly on the senses than a quick wham-bam-thank-you-ma'am! And this dress,' he mused quietly as he slipped one of the shoestring straps over her shoulder, 'is far too lovely to be ripped off.'

'Dominic—'

'Mmm?'

She had meant to plead with him. To tell him to put her out of her misery. To do it quickly and get it over with. Because the long, slow, erotic coupling she suspected he had in mind was far too dangerous to contemplate. For how could she contain herself and not blurt out the ridiculously soppy words of love she was longing to say to him?

'What is it, Romy?' he questioned.

Romy swallowed, aware that whatever she had *meant* to say to him it was now too late, because he was sliding the other strap of her dress down.

She shuddered in wonder as he began to peel the bodice down over the lush swell of her breasts, laying them bare to his rapidly dilating eyes.

'Not wearing a bra, I see,' he murmured approvingly. 'That was very naughty of you, Romy. Did you think that it would save time?' He dipped his head to dart his tongue out at one exquisitely hardened nipple, and Romy let out a little cry of satisfaction.

'I do hope you bothered to put some panties on,' he whispered as his hand roved experimentally over her satin-covered thigh. He rucked up the material with a practised hand until he was able to slide his fingers to the top of her thigh. And when he allowed them to brush against the lace and satin Romy almost wept with delight.

'Oh, you *are* wearing some,' he observed. 'That's good. Would you like me to take them off now, or shall we wait? Or shall we leave them on, perhaps? Just push that little scrap of fabric aside and let me drive deep into you. What do you say to that, Romy?'

She was powerless to speak; he could have done anything he wanted to right then, her body thrilling to every new touch and caress.

Dominic was slightly surprised by her passive capitulation, even as he revelled in watching her respond to his mouth and his hands, and very soon his...

He swallowed down his excitement. He had expected...what? That once Romy had accepted that he meant to make love to her all night long then maybe she would demonstrate every erotic little variation on the act she must have learned over the years?

And yet this strangely innocent reaction—so at odds with her previous behaviour—was oddly thrilling. He had her entirely in the palm of his hand. And never had a woman made him feel at once so powerful and yet so vulnerable.

He found the zip to her gown and slid it down, pleased when he could finally peel the garment from her body and let it slither to the carpet.

She lay there wearing nothing but her panties, her stockings and suspenders and her high-heeled bronze shoes, and Dominic had to fight very hard with himself not to take her as quickly and as brutally as he had just vowed not to.

Sucking in a deep, hot breath of air, he managed to compose himself enough to rip the black bow-tie from his neck and drop it on top of her dress.

Romy's eyelids fluttered slightly.

She was watching him; he knew that. And normally, given how much she wanted him, he would have taken great pleasure in demonstrating his control by taking as long as possible to remove his clothes.

But suddenly his control had flown, and he was not sure that he was *able* to tease her by stripping, even if he wanted to.

Because Dominic was suddenly overwhelmed by the most primitive sensation he had ever experienced, which went way beyond reason or even desire.

He wanted to possess her. To penetrate her. To impale and impregnate her... Dominic swallowed back his desire with an effort, and two mother-of-pearl buttons skittered over the floor as he pulled his dress shirt off with an impatient yank.

Romy saw some kind of struggle taking place on his devilishly handsome features. She didn't understand it, but it touched some deep, hidden core in her. And she was unable to resist doing what she had wanted to do for so long now. She wound her arms sinuously around his neck and kissed him.

The kiss was like a lightning bolt shooting through his veins, and Dominic almost exploded with need. As unco-ordinated as a young boy on his first sexual exploration, he felt his fingers had never disobeyed him quite so much.

And then Romy began to help him, wiggling her toes so that she could help kick his shoes off. Still in her scanty bits of underwear, she bent to peel a black silk sock off each foot while Dominic struggled to pull his zip down over his ever-growing hardness—terrified that he might emasculate himself into the bargain.

When he was finally naked, Romy began to have second thoughts about the sofa. He seemed so wonderful—so excited and enchanted by her—that her fears over comparisons seemed strangely redundant.

He removed her panties more roughly than he had intended, and then moved to lie over her, but he must have sensed her uncertainty, for he paused and looked deep into her eyes and said, 'What is it?'

'If you want to go upstairs, I don't mind.'

Dominic thought how ironic it was that when she spoke in that sweet, little-girl way she sounded almost *virginal*. He shook his head regretfully. 'Afterwards,' he promised. 'If I try to take you up there now, we're going to end up doing it on the stairs. And I can't wait any longer, Romy, sweetheart—'

She heard the break in his voice as he began to thrust into her, all raw, virile, masculine power, and then the glaze of passion which had darkened his face in anticipation became one of horrified disbelief.

'Dear *God*, Romy!' he exclaimed in a strangled voice as the barrier he had only ever read about before made itself felt to him. 'Why the hell didn't you *tell* me?'

CHAPTER EIGHT

'DON'T stop,' begged Romy, not caring how desperate she sounded. Because if he stopped now she would die. 'Please don't stop, Dominic.'

She could see the indecision which darkened his features, and her body clenched with fear.

But the movement seemed to excite him, for he closed his eyes briefly, as if in despair, before beginning to move again. This time he broke through the barrier, and as he saw the tears which slid down from beneath her tightly closed eyes he could have cursed himself.

'Did I hurt you?' he whispered.

'Only a little.' And oh, if that was pain then she wanted a lifetime of it.

He stared down at her as he moved. Romy was a *virgin*! Dominic shook his head again in disbelief. And that was his last coherent thought as he began to employ every bit of skill and finesse he had ever learned.

He had never slept with a virgin before, but he knew that it was notoriously difficult for a woman to achieve orgasm during her first experience of sexual intercourse.

Never had it been so important to please a woman, and never had it been more difficult.

Dominic couldn't ever remember struggling to hold

back like this before—not even on his own very first encounter.

Emotionally, he felt as out of his depth as a sixteen-year-old, yet physically he was determined to make this the most fabulous experience of her life.

He watched as her body relaxed and accommodated his. He observed with fascination and absorption the physical signs of her flowering, seeing the delicious flush of rose-pink as it transformed the creamy lushness of her skin.

He moved slowly, revelling in each deep, agonisingly blissful thrust for immeasurable moments, until at last he sensed that she was on the very brink.

And then, only then, did he allow himself to become engulfed in the pleasure too, so that loss of control had never been quite so sweet or quite so poignant.

His last thought was that he had not given even a second of consideration to the question of contraception. But somehow he didn't care, and even if he did it was now too late, and they both fell over the top, their cries the only sound echoing around the vast room.

Romy found herself completely engulfed in the aftermath. She was filled with the most delicious glow. Swamped by it.

She tightened her arms around Dominic's bare back as it rose and fell with the effort of dragging air back into his lungs. She felt the gradual slowing of his heart and the infinitely pleasurable sensation of his spasms as they stilled deep inside her.

But then he levered himself up onto his elbows, his face dark with some unnamed emotion as he withdrew from her.

A stranger.

Romy shivered as the afterglow began to wear away. She became aware that she was lying almost naked on the sofa—still wearing her shoes and stockings, with her legs sprawled out all over the place.

He reached out an arm and retrieved his dress shirt, tossed it to her and said harshly, 'Put this on.'

Shakily, she complied, her heart sinking as he got to his feet and pulled on his trousers, then moved to the fireplace where he stood, his face taking on the unmoving expression of a statue. Only his eyes glittered with life.

'How?' he said simply.

Romy shook her head. 'Does it matter?'

He clenched his fists involuntarily by his sides. 'Of course it *matters*!' he ground out. 'Or did you imagine that I would simply overlook the fact that I was the first man for you?' He forced himself to extinguish the possessive thrill that just saying those words gave him. 'Even though you were married for over three years!'

Romy bit her lip in confusion. Her dilemma lay in whether to honour the living—or the dead.

Dominic stared at her. 'How?' he asked again.

Telling him was no guarantee of happiness, and Romy had been hurt too badly to risk it. 'I'm sure you have ideas of your own, Dominic,' she answered flippantly.

Black, warring thoughts crowded his mind.

Nameless fears which begged to be recognised. 'Oh, sure,' he answered coldly. 'No shortage of those.'

'Oh?'

Oh, the way she lay there, he thought, suppressing a groan. So beautiful and so damned erotic, the half-buttoned dress shirt giving him the occasional provocative glimpse of her silken stockings with those tantalising strips of bare flesh above. 'Was that why Mark excluded you from his inheritance?' he demanded.

Romy sighed. 'He excluded me from his inheritance because I asked him to.'

Black brows were raised in a look which was frankly disbelieving. 'Oh, *really*?'

'Yes, really.' Dominic's contempt stirred her in a way that his indifference would never have done. Because the dark inner struggle which was taking place on those cold, beautiful features was surely some sort of indication that he cared? Did she dare to let herself hope?

'There was very little inheritance in any case,' she told him calmly. 'The estate is all tied up for future generations. Mark's brother's son will inherit. And the remainder—the fairly modest amount of cash and jewels—well, that was needed to pay for Mark's mother's nursing. She's infirm now, and needs ~~round the-clock care.~~'

'Yes, I know,' he said bleakly, and turned a piercing silver gaze on her. 'And all that is admirable of you, Romy—but I'm still no closer to understanding why—'

'We didn't consummate our marriage?' Romy looked down at her ringless hands.

'Precisely.'

Romy thought of Mark and the comfort she had offered him. Of the long, dark nights when she had held his hand to try to ward off his fears. Able to give him in that small way what he had been unable to take from her in any other...

She looked up at Dominic, her eyes suddenly wet, her face a mass of confusion. 'It's Mark's story,' she said.

'And Mark is *dead*!' he lashed back, almost viciously.

'Yes.' Mark was dead. And Mark had loved her, in so much as he had been capable of loving anyone. The very last thing he had said to her before he died had been, 'Be happy, Romy. Promise me.'

And she had replied in a voice choked with tears, 'I promise.'

'I never slept with Mark before we were married,' she began slowly.

'That became very apparent just a short while ago,' Dominic clipped back, his eyes hooded and suspicious.

Romy swallowed. 'He told me that it was because he loved me and respected me—which was why he wanted to wait until we were married.'

'Go on.'

'I knew that wasn't the way that most people these days behaved, but in a way I was glad to wait.' Romy swallowed. 'It seemed an indication of how much he cared for me. And also...'

Dominic frowned as he heard her voice quaver. 'Yes?'

'It reassured me that I *wanted* to wait, too. That I was not desperate to leap into bed with him. That I was not as promiscuous as my...as my...'

'As your mother?' he guessed suddenly, and it was as though a curtain before his eyes had been lifted.

'Yes.' Romy did up another button of the shirt almost absently, not noticing that Dominic's eyes followed the movement obsessively. 'Then I met you. In the lift. And, well...you know what happened next.'

She scrubbed at her eyes furiously with the back of her fist, and Dominic had to quash the urge to go across and take her in his arms once more.

'Yes,' he said, in a grim voice. 'I know what happened next—it has haunted me ever since, Romy.'

'And me too!' she retorted fiercely. 'Or do you really think that I did that kind of thing with every good-looking man I bumped into? Well? Do you?'

He didn't give it a moment's thought. 'No,' he answered. 'I don't think that.'

She quickly brushed a tear away. 'I went back to my room that day. I don't know what I planned to do—maybe talk to my mother, except that she had passed out cold on the bed. And then Mark came by and I...' She looked up, the truth written in her dark eyes, and Dominic recoiled as though she had hit him.

'You *told* him?' he queried incredulously. 'You told Mark?'

'Yes, of course I told him.'

'Just *what*, exactly,' he demanded, his eyes glittering dangerously, 'did you tell him?'

Romy swallowed. 'I told him that we had been—intimate. That if circumstances had been different we probably would have ended up making love. I didn't go into details about what we had actually done.'

'Thank God for that!' uttered Dominic quietly.

'I gave him the opportunity to call the wedding off, but he wouldn't hear of it. He blamed himself, saying that he had put me in that position by not...' She took a deep, painful breath. 'By not making love to me himself. He told me that you were the type of man who had always had hundreds of lovers, and that even if I called off the wedding you wouldn't be interested in me for more than a night.'

'Oh, *did* he?' asked Dominic, in a quiet, emotionless voice.

She knotted her whitened knuckles together. 'He begged and pleaded with me to stay with him, and to marry him.'

'And you agreed?' he queried incredulously. 'You *agreed*?'

Her eyes were dark and curiously empty. 'Yes, I agreed,' she told him sadly. 'But I was young, Dominic. Frightened and guilty and confused. And I wanted to escape. Mark knew that—he played on my weaknesses, while I confess that I allowed him to. And I was nothing if not optimistic. I convinced myself that on our wedding night my love and affection for Mark would be enough to obliterate every memory of you.'

'But it didn't happen?'

Romy shook her head. 'No, it didn't. We didn't

make love on our wedding night, nor on any other night.'

'Mark didn't want to?'

'Mark couldn't,' she told him bluntly. 'Mark was impotent.'

He let out a long, tortured sigh. 'Dear God,' he said to himself bitterly. 'And when did you discover this, Romy?'

She swallowed. 'On our wedding night, actually. He told me then.'

Dominic's eyes narrowed with suppressed rage. 'He was prepared to do *that* to you? To begin a marriage knowing that it might never be consummated?'

Romy stared at him, wide-eyed. She had never thought about it in those terms before. 'He told me that he had never had any interest in sex, but he was too frightened to go to the doctor about it. And when eventually he did, soon after we were married, we discovered that he had very little time left.'

'And of course you couldn't leave him then?' he guessed.

'Of course I couldn't,' said Romy. 'And he didn't want me to.'

'Emotional blackmail,' said Dominic heavily.

'Oh, it was a lot more complex than you make it sound, Dominic. In a way, I felt it was the least I could do after betraying him—and with his best friend, too. I was at least in part responsible for the ending of your friendship. And it wasn't as bad as it sounds—I *liked* Mark. I always had done. Staying with him was not an awful prison—I was glad to be able to help him. And besides,' she finished miserably, 'I had nowhere else to go.'

There was a long silence, before Dominic said, 'I see,' in an odd, final sort of voice, and Romy decided that she would leave with her pride intact. Before he kicked her out.

She rose stiffly to her feet, longing to go upstairs and get changed. The white shirt she wore was full of his scent and unbearably evocative, reminding her with heart-rending clarity of just how beautifully he had made love to her.

'I'd better go,' she said, and he frowned.

'Go where?'

'Home. Anywhere. Away from here, in any case.'

He had taken on the watchful pose of someone deciding how best to break in a young horse.

She strode towards the door, aware that she must look ridiculous in a thigh-length shirt and a pair of high-heeled shoes.

'Walk out of here now, Romy Salisbury, and you walk out of my life for good,' came his grated comment from behind her.

Romy whirled round, searching his face for clues. 'But what alternative do I have?'

'The alternative is that you stay.'

But what was he offering her? A wonderful love affair? Would that be enough for her? Romy wondered. Would she be prepared to settle for that when she wanted so much more?

'But there is, of course, a condition to your staying,' he continued, still in that same, rather emotionless voice.

And this was the pay-off. Romy wondered just how he would word it. Would he insist on laying down ground rules right from the beginning? Insist that she must make no demands on him? That she must always be there for him?

Romy bristled. Well, he could keep all those conditions, and she would tell him exactly where he could put them!

She fixed a saccharine smile to her face. 'Oh? And what's that?'

'That you'll try one day to find it in your heart to love me almost as much as I love you,' he told her gently.

There was a long, stunned silence.

'Oh, Dominic!' she wailed, and burst into tears. 'I *do* love you—I always have! I've thought about no one else but you, since the day I met you! And you didn't even realise—you stupid, *stupid* man!' she sobbed.

He pulled her into his arms and let her cry. She soaked his bare chest, and then he found a handkerchief in the top pocket of his discarded jacket and very tenderly wiped her face with it.

And only when she had stopped snuffling did he allow himself to smile, and to kiss the end of her nose with all the sloppiness he normally despised in other people but which now—most extraordinarily—he found he wanted to indulge in for the rest of his life!

'Am I really stupid?' he queried softly.

'*Yes!*'

'So I suppose marriage is out of the question, then?'

She eyed him suspiciously. 'If you think *that*, Dominic Dashwood,' she declared, 'then you really *are* stupid!'

He smiled again at her baffling lack of logic. 'Soon?'

'I don't mind. Just so long as we can live together first.'

'It had better be soon,' he told her sternly. 'Since we have just made love without using any form of contraception.'

'Gosh!' Romy felt quite dizzy with pride. 'So we did.' Then she frowned. 'Are you normally quite so careless?'

Dominic hid a smile. He was not used to being told off by a woman. He rather liked it. 'Never,' he told her honestly. 'But I just assumed that you were on the Pill—and please don't look like that, Romy; you have to agree that it was a perfectly reasonable assumption to make, under the circumstances.'

'I suppose so,' she sighed, and kissed the gravelly shadow of his chin. 'But what if I had had millions of partners before you?'

He stared deep into her eyes. 'Do you know—the thought of using contraception as a protective device with you simply never occurred to me? And I've never, ever taken that risk before.'

'So why do something so out of character with me? Someone who you would have been justified in protecting yourself against, given all the evidence?'

'Because I wasn't acting on evidence; I was acting on instinct,' he told her lovingly. 'Maybe I knew, deep in my heart, that the only risk I was taking was having my heart broken into the bargain!'

No chance of *that*! thought Romy.

'In fact,' he mused, 'if we're talking about carelessness, I *could* wonder why you didn't bother telling me that you were a virgin…?' He raised his dark brows at her questioningly.

Romy sighed. 'I guess I wanted to get my own back. You thought that I was a raving nymphomaniac, and I wanted to prove to you that I wasn't.'

'Revenge in its sweetest form?' he questioned.

'You could say that.'

'But rather a dramatic way of going about it.'

'You bring out the worst in me, Dominic,' she murmured, but he shook his head.

'The very best,' he demurred.

Well, she wasn't going to argue with *that*! 'And also,' she admitted, 'I was terribly afraid that if you knew I was a virgin you would insist on doing the honourable thing.'

'The "honourable thing" being?'

Romy shrugged. 'You know. Insisting on me staying pure and unsullied, and not making love to me.'

He grinned. 'I may have honourable traits, sweetheart, but I'm not *completely* stupid!' He narrowed his eyes, as if a thought had suddenly occurred to him. 'That—um—divine experience in the garden… How in heaven's name did a virgin learn how to do *that*?'

'She used her imagination,' Romy told him smugly. 'I happen to have a *very* vivid imagination, you know, Dominic!'

His eyes darkened. 'Shall we go to bed now?' he growled.

'Oh, yes, *please*,' she sighed happily. 'And can we do it again?'

Dominic laughed aloud, feeling more light-hearted than he could ever remember feeling. 'As often as you like, sweetheart—as often as you like.'

He suddenly noticed the telephone receiver lying on the floor by the sofa. 'Oh, dear—one of us must have kicked it off,' he observed drily, loving the way she blushed so sweetly.

He replaced it onto the handset and it trilled out almost immediately. Romy listened while he said, 'Mmm. Mmm. When? Good. That's good! Yes. Yes, she is.' And finally, 'I'm getting married. Yes! Of course it's to Romy. We'll tell you all about it. Tomorrow?' He grinned at Romy. 'Well, maybe not tomorrow—I have the strongest suspicion we're going to be very tied up for the next few days! I'll phone you.'

He put the receiver down, looking very slightly bemused. 'That was Triss,' he explained. 'Archie has been trying to get through to us, but couldn't—so he rang her and Cormack instead. He and Dolly arrived at the hospital just as their daughter-in-law produced a baby girl—she's quite small but absolutely perfect! And they are both doing well.'

'Oh, Dominic,' said Romy breathlessly. 'Isn't that just fantastic?'

'It is.' He smiled indulgently. 'In fact, everything is.'

'Just one other thing.' She pursed her lips together as he lifted her into his arms.

'Mmm?'

'How on earth did Triss know that you were going to marry *me*?'

He smiled. 'Before the party, I told her that I wanted to get you out of my system.'

'And was that why you brought me here?' she quizzed softly.

'I'm afraid it was.' His expression was rueful and his eyes were as silver as the moonlit lake outside. 'But it went even further than that. You hit the nail on the head when you accused me of wanting to make you fall in love with me, sweetheart. I did. But I didn't question my motives for doing so too closely.

'You see, Romy, I thought that following an appropriate period of mourning you would come looking for me after Mark died. And when you didn't...I...'

'What?' she whispered, thinking of the countless times she had lifted the telephone to contact him, and replaced it again, not daring to risk his contemptuous rejection.

'I felt used,' he admitted. 'No better than a stud you'd got a cheap thrill from. I couldn't forget you—in fact, the memory of you was making it impossible for me to live any kind of normal life. And so I plotted to bring you here—wanting you to be ensnared by me so that I could inflict on you the same kind of suffering and torment I had been forced to endure while you were away from me.'

'Revenge?' mused Romy.

'Revenge,' he echoed, and his face darkened. 'But for once I lacked the perception to see that *I* was still totally ensnared by *you*.' He looked at her candidly, a wry smile curving his lips. 'And I never thought that when love came it would hit me like that.'

'Like what?' she asked him, intrigued.

'Like a thunderbolt. Sudden. Powerful. Irrational.' His eyes glittered. 'And all-consuming. That kind of wild, crazy love seemed too much part of the world I had grown up in, where instant gratification was everything. The world I had wanted to escape so badly.'

'And how did you think that love would come, Dominic?' she asked him softly.

'Oh, slow...and considered. And carefully evaluated.' He smiled. 'Deadly dull, in fact.'

He picked her hand up and slowly kissed each finger in turn, and Romy thrilled at the expression of wonder in his eyes.

'I also told Triss that I had an old score to settle with you.'

'And what did she say?'

'Just that I was straying into dangerous waters—that she knew from her own experiences that revenge has an awful habit of backfiring on you. And it has,' he finished, on a whisper, 'in the most delightful way imaginable.'

'Oh, Dominic,' sighed Romy, her heart almost bursting. 'I love you very much.'

'Then show me, sweetheart,' he said, and his voice was suddenly urgent. 'Show me.'

*   *   *

'And I now pronounce you man and wife.' The registrar beamed when—as if on cue—a blackbird began to sing its heart out in one of the trees. 'You may now kiss the bride,' he said.

Dominic needed no second bidding. He bent his head and briefly brushed Romy's lips, their eyes meeting in a long, long smile which excluded the rest of the world.

And then came the low buzz of conversation as the guests all began to chatter excitedly.

'Not a very passionate kiss,' whispered Lola rather disappointedly. She had been hoping for a passionate clinch in the manner of Rhett and Scarlett! 'And certainly not what you would expect from Dominic Dashwood—not with *his* reputation!'

'I rather suspect,' answered Geraint drily, 'that Dominic is holding back—and that if he *really* kissed her he might get completely carried away. Did you see that look he gave her just now? Positively X-rated!'

Lola screwed up her blue eyes. 'I see what you mean,' she whispered delightedly. 'Look at the way they're gazing at each other now—they look as lovestruck as two teenagers!'

Geraint laughed, and gave her a look of mock despair as he pulled her into his arms. 'And do you still gaze at me that way, my love?'

Lola looked smug, remembering the way he had ravished her on the bed just an hour earlier—nearly making them late for the wedding! 'I look at you that way all the time, Geraint Howell-Williams—as well you know.'

Geraint laughed, just as Cormack and Triss wandered over. Cormack had a sleeping baby in a stripy suit flopped contentedly over his shoulder, while Triss was wearing fuchsia-coloured satin trousers, which were skin-tight, with a matching matador jacket whose orange buttons matched her outrageous hat.

'The Italian designer?' guessed Lola.

Triss grinned. 'Spot on! Completely over the top, isn't it? But I love his clothes, and I'd feel guilty about paying shop prices for them.'

'And fortunately I love them, too,' said Cormack, his eyes glinting as he gazed adoringly at his wife. 'I shall never forget that excuse for a skirt you wore on our honeymoon! The gondolier almost fell head first into the canal! Remember?'

'Mmm.' Triss had seen far less of the canals and treasures of Venice than she had expected, but she knew every single centimetre of their rooms at the Cipriani! They really would have to go back and visit when they *weren't* on honeymoon!

'We only *just* got married before Romy and Dominic, didn't we?' said Triss, looking dreamily into her husband's eyes. 'And we've known each other for ages longer.'

'It wasn't through a lack of asking,' growled Cormack.

'I just like keeping you guessing,' answered his wife sweetly as she planted a tender kiss on the top of their baby's silky black head.

'And what are you keeping me guessing about this time, I wonder?' queried Cormack softly.

'Guess!' She smiled, but she could see from the

look in his eyes that he already knew she was pregnant with their second child.

'I love you, Triss,' he whispered.

'The feeling is entirely mutual, I can assure you.'

The bride and groom had wandered hand in hand through the rose-decked arbour and out towards the lake.

Romy wore the simplest dress in cream silk, which brushed the grass as she walked, and a circlet of matching cream roses on top of her blonde head.

The sun dazzled off the mirror-smooth surface of the water and their senses were full of music and laughter and birdsong.

They stood in silence for a while, both lost in thought, reflecting on their good fortune and happiness. Then Dominic turned and looked at his wife, experiencing the usual thrill of pride and pleasure.

'Happy?'

'Mmm. Unbelievably so.'

'But you're very quiet,' he probed. 'Are you sad because your mother couldn't make it?'

'*Wouldn't* make it, you mean,' Romy corrected him drily, but her words were totally without anger. Dominic had taught her that when you couldn't change something it was sometimes best just to accept it.

She shook her head. 'No, I'm not sad. I'm glad she's happy with her new man, and if she *had* come she probably would have done something totally outrageous—like making a speech or jumping into the swimming pool fully clothed!'

'So why are you so reflective? Were you thinking about Mark?'

Her eyes shone with tears at his perception, and she nodded.

He cupped her face in his strong hand. 'Don't be sad, sweetheart. Mark's out of pain now. And today you kept your promise to him in the fullest sense. You told him that you would be happy, and you *are* going to be happy. I'm going to spend the rest of my life making that promise come true.'

Ever since that night two months ago, when they had come together so passionately, Romy had sometimes felt that she was going to *burst* with happiness!

But Dominic was right, and it was time to let the past go now. Time to let go of any lingering regrets and guilt.

On an impulse, Romy scooped the circlet of roses off her head and tossed it into the lake, like a discus. The gleaming water parted and rippled as the flowers hit the surface, and the sun gilded the cream petals. She said a short, silent prayer for Mark, and bade him farewell, then lovingly turned her face up to her husband.

Dominic squeezed her hand tightly. 'OK now?'

'OK.' She smiled, and looked down at her posy of cream roses which she was still clutching tightly to her chest.

Dominic shot her a brief glance. 'Want to go back to the reception and toss your bouquet in traditional fashion?'

What Romy *wanted* was to have her gorgeous new husband all to herself, but she had the rest of her life for that, and she thought she could *possibly* share him. Just for today!

She turned to him with a grin. 'But there's no one left to get married, is there? Lola and Geraint. Triss and Cormack. And now us.'

Dominic frowned. 'What about that friend of yours? The rather attractive one with dark hair?'

'Stephanie? She'll be delighted to hear that you described her as attractive.'

'But a little miserable, I think?'

'She's just broken up with her boyfriend.'

'Ah! Then she sounds the perfect bouquet recipient to me. Come on, sweetheart.'

He took her by the hand, but she halted and turned her big brown eyes up to him.

'Kiss me first, Dominic!'

'Romy,' he warned, because he knew that look very well.

'Just a kiss,' she pouted.

'With you it's never *just* a kiss. Oh, come here, then.' He sighed, on a note midway between passion and perplexity. 'Why is it that I can never resist you?' he wondered aloud. 'I'm like putty in your hands, do you know that, Romy Dashwood?'

'Oh, *that*!' Romy's eyes sparkled. 'That's called love!' And the bouquet slid unnoticed to the ground.

Dominic sighed with pleasure as he kissed her very thoroughly, and she slid her hands beneath his jacket to encircle his waist. 'Romy!' he groaned.

'What, darling?' she questioned innocently, her fingertips massaging his broad back through the silk of his shirt.

Dominic knew when he was beaten—but more importantly, he knew when he *wanted* to be beaten.

He was laughing with delight as he tumbled her down onto the grass and began to kiss her.

Presents Extravaganza
25 YEARS!

Harlequin Presents® will make it even
easier to pick up a Presents title—
and you'll be glad you did!

As an added bonus you can save
$1.00 off the purchase of your next
Harlequin Presents® book!

Take 4 bestselling love stories FREE

Plus get a FREE surprise gift!

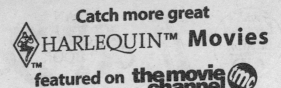

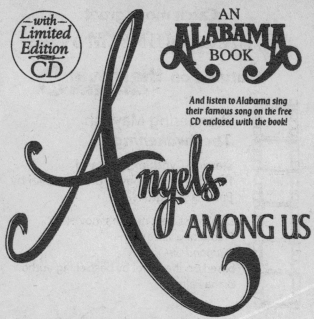
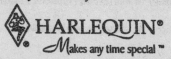

Presents Extravaganza
25 YEARS!

**With the purchase of two Harlequin Presents®
books, you can send in for a FREE Silvertone Book
Pendant. Retail value $19.95. It's our gift to you!**

FREE SILVERTONE BOOK PENDANT

On the official proof-of-purchase coupon below, fill in your name,
address and zip or postal code, and send it, plus $1.50 U.S./
$2.50 CAN. for postage and handling, (check or money order—please
do not send cash), to Harlequin books: In the U.S.: 3010 Walden
Avenue, P.O. Box 9077, Buffalo, N.Y. 14269-9077; In Canada: P.O. Box
609, Fort Erie, Ontario L2A 5X3. Please allow 4-6 weeks for delivery.
Order your Silvertone Book Pendant now! Quantities are limited. Offer
for the FREE Silvertone Book Pendant expires December 31, 1998.

Harlequin Presents®
Extravaganza!

Official Proof of Purchase
"Please send me a FREE Silvertone Book Pendant."

Name: _____

Address: _____

City: _____

State/Prov.: _____ Zip/Postal Code: _____

Reader Service Account: _____

 HARLEQUIN®   097 KGP CSAY 716-1

HP25POP

Coming Next Month

HARLEQUIN PRESENTS®

THE BEST HAS JUST GOTTEN BETTER!

#1959 SINFUL PLEASURES Anne Mather
Megan was back in San Felipe to find that much had changed.
Her stepsister's son, Remy, had been nine to her fifteen when
she saw him last—now he was a deeply attractive man. And
Megan sensed danger.

#1960 THE MARRIAGE CAMPAIGN Helen Bianchin
Dominic wanted Francesca, and he'd planned a very special
campaign for winning her. She may be wary of loving again,
but he was going to pursue, charm and seduce her
relentlessly—until she said yes!

#1961 THE SECRET WIFE Lynne Graham
Nothing could have prepared Rosie for Greek tycoon
Constantine Voulos—or his insistence that she marry him! But
she soon realized she couldn't just be his temporary wife. Her
secret would have to be told!

#1962 THE DIVORCÉE SAID YES! Sandra Marton
(The Wedding of the Year)
When Chase suggested to ex-wife, Annie, that they pretend to
get back together to reassure their daughter that love could
last, Annie was amazed. But then she found herself agreeing
to his plan....

#1963 ULTIMATE TEMPTATION Sara Craven
(Nanny Wanted!)
Count Giulio Falcone needed a nanny to look after his sister's
children. Lucy was in his debt *and* in his house. Suddenly she
found herself in the wrong place at the wrong time, with the
ultimate temptation—Giulio!

#1964 GIRL TROUBLE Sandra Field
(Man Talk)
Cade loved Lori, but she had two daughters—one of whom
had taken an instant dislike to him. He only wanted one
blonde in his life, not three. Trouble was, getting Lori into his
bed meant accepting the little girls into his heart!